Hauntings

OTHER TITLES FROM KATHA

FOR LITERARY CONNOISSEURS
Katha Prize Stories, vols 1-9
 ed Geeta Dharmarajan
A Southern Harvest ed Githa Hariharan
Visions-Revisions, vols 1-2
 ed Keerti Ramachandra
The Wordsmiths ed Meenakshi Sharma
Masti ed Ramachandra Sharma
Basheer ed Vanajam Ravindran
Mauni ed Lakshmi Holmström
Raja Rao ed Makarand Paranjape
Mapping Memories ed Sukrita Paul Kumar
 and Muhammad Ali Siddiqui
Separate Journeys ed Geeta Dharmarajan
Sleepwalkers ed Keerti Ramachandra
The Essence of Camphor: Naiyer Masud
 ed Muhammad Umar Memon
Word as Mantra: The Art of Raja Rao
 ed Robert L Hardgrave, Jr
Imaging the Other
 ed GJV Prasad and Sara Rai
Ambai ed Gita Krishnankutty
Ismat: Her Life, Her Times ed Sukrita Paul
 Kumar and Sadique

EASY READERS FOR ADULT NEO-LITERATES (IN HINDI)
Abhishaap by Pudhuvai Rā Rajani
Arjun by Mahaswetaa Devi
Bhola by Rajendra Singh Bedi
Do Haath by Ismat Chughtai
Faisla by Maitreyi Pushpa
Panch Parmeshwar by Premchand
Paro ki Kahani by Sughra Mehdi
Puraskar by Jaishankar Prasad
Samudra Tat Par by O V Vijayan
Sparsh by Jaywant Dalvi
Stree ka Patra by Rabindranath Tagore
Thakavat by Gurbachan Singh Bhullar
Stree Katha (a teaching/learning text,
 also in Gujarati, Kannada, Malayalam,
 Telugu & Urdu)

Stree Shakti (a teaching/learning text,
 also in English, Kannada & Malayalam)

FOR YOUNG ADULTS
*A Unique Odyssey: The Story of the United
 Nations* Geeta Dharmarajan
The Nose Doctor ed Rosalind Wilson
The Carpenter's Apprentice ed Rosalind Wilson
The YuvaKatha Series I to VI
 ed Geeta Dharmarajan and
 Keerti Ramachandra

FOR CHILDREN
Hulgul ka Pitara (a teaching/learning
 kit for Hindi)
Tamasha! (a fun & development
 magazine in English & Hindi)
Dhammak Dhum! (a magazine for pre-
 schoolers)
*Swapnasundari and the Magical Birds
 of Mithila* (in English & Hindi)
*The Secrets of Kalindi: A Jigsaw Puzzle
 Mystery*
The Princesss with the Longest Hair
 (winner of the ChitraKala Award)

FORTHCOMING
Ayoni & other stories
 ed Alladi Uma and M Sridhar
Katha Prize Stories, vol 10
 ed Geeta Dharmarajan

KATHA ACADEMIC SERIES:
APPROACHES TO LITERATURE IN TRANSLATION (ALT)
Partition Narratives ed Ravikant and
 Tarun Saint
Caste Consciousness and Indian Fiction
 ed Tapan Basu
Translating Desire ed Brinda Bose
Women and Space ed C T Indra and
 Meenakshi Shivaram

Hauntings
Bangla Ghost Stories

translated and edited by
Suchitra Samanta

Katha Regional Fiction Series

Published by

KATHA

A-3 Sarvodaya Enclave
Sri Aurobindo Marg, New Delhi 110017
Phone: 686 8193, 652 1752
Fax: 651 4373
E-mail: katha@vsnl.com
Internet address: http://www.katha.org

Published by Katha in May, 2000

Copyright © Katha, May, 2000

Copyright © for each individual story in its original language is held by the author. Copyright © for "Khhudita Pashan," "Manihara," and "Nishithe," by Rabindranath Tagore, and for "Ahuti" by Pramatha Chaudhuri, is held by Visva Bharati. Copyright © for the English translations rests with KATHA.

KATHA is a registered nonprofit society devoted to enhancing the pleasures of reading. KATHA VILASAM is its story research and resource centre.

In-house Editors: Aparajita Basu, Chandana Dutta, Nandita Aggarwal, Shoma Choudhury
Cover Design: Geeta Dharmarajan, Arvinder Chawla
Book Design: Arvinder Chawla
Production-in-charge: S Ganeshan

Typeset in 11 on 15.5pt ElegaGarmnd BT by Sandeep Kumar
at Katha and Printed at Param Offsetters, New Delhi

Katha books are distributed in India through
KATHAMELA
distributors of quality books.
A-3 Sarvodaya Enclave, Sri Aurobindo Marg, New Delhi 110 017

All rights reserved. No part of this book may be reproduced or utilized in any form or by any means, electronic or mechanical, including photocopying, recording or by any information storage or retrieval system, without the prior written permission of the publisher.

ISBN 81-87649-01-1

Contents

Acknowledgements

Introduction

At Dead of Night, 15
  RABINDRANATH TAGORE

The Hungering Stones, 31
  RABINDRANATH TAGORE

Manihara, 47
  RABINDRANATH TAGORE

Sacrifice by Fire, 69
  PRAMATHA CHAUDHURI

The Poet's Lover, 89
  PANCHKARI DE

In the Forest of Bomaiburu, 109
  BIBHUTIBHUSHAN BANDOPADHYAY

The Witch, 119
  TARASHANKAR BANDOPADHYAY

Giribala, 139
BANAPHUL

Nightcall, 147
SWAPANBURO

Chimaera, 157
LILA MAJUMDAR

The Lady of the House, 167
KAMAKSHIPRASAD CHATTOPADHYAY

Wedding Night, 177
SHISHIR LAHIRI

In the Forests of Jharowa, 197
MAHASWETA DEVI

Notes on Contributors

Acknowledgements

Many have contributed to this anthology, in different ways. My grateful thanks to Associate Professor Susan McKinnon at the Department of Anthropology, University of Virginia, for her enthusiasm when I first mentioned this project to her; to Professor Karen Prazniak at the Department of History, Hampden-Syden College, for her comments on the first few translations; to my good friend Dr Leslie Furlong, fellow anthropologist, for her thoughtful response to the complete manuscript; to Dr Anna Lawson, Dr Mary Atwell and to Ms Lucy Lee, members of my lively book discussion group who were interested, curious and delighted by the stories, and whose insights helped me with writing the Introduction; to Professor Cathy Hankla, Chair of the English Department at Hollins University, who gave me valuable advice about writing to publishers; and to my cousin Tina and her husband Micheal Webb for their advice about the technicalities of publication, and for their support and affection.

My special thanks too to my family – my daughter Shahana for her lively and intelligent interest; my father for pointing me to certain stories; and my husband Shivaji for his computer expertise, which facilitated the editing of the manuscript, and its moving electronically (virus free!) between the USA and Delhi.

This book is dedicated to my husband Shivaji, my daughter Shahana (Tuki), my father Sushil Kumar Bardhan Ray, and to the memory of my mother Surabala Bardhan Ray – with love.

Introduction

This collection of thirteen stories on ghosts, witches, vampires and other supernatural entities is only a very small selection from a vast opus on the topic from Bengal – an opus that includes folktales, stories for children, stories for more adult readers, as well as renowned literary classics in the genre. My selection of the stories for this anthology was guided by several criteria.

For one, I selected those that were well-written, namely, I looked for fluidity in expression, depth in characterization, complexity of plot, and above all, stories that moved the imagination – where fluidity, depth, complexity and imagination are integrally related. In other words, I omitted stories that, while interesting to read, at best only described some supernatural "event." I also omitted stories which though well-written were similar in theme to others in the anthology.

I selected these stories primarily because they featured women as protagonists. While I did not start this project with that intention, I discovered that some of the best stories – mostly written by men – portrayed wonderfully the complex emotions that drive women. In this context, those emotions – of jealousy, greed, the hunger for youth, unrequited love, rage, revenge, attachment – were expressed uniquely, variously and powerfully – from beyond the pale of the everyday. Further, this anthology offers some insight into the gendered aspect of the supernatural in Bengali culture, and therefore "real" women, in Bengali belief. Where the general term bhoot, ghost, also includes in its connotation both "passions" as well as "material substance," the emotions of the protagonists in these stories find passionate expression by means of their supernatural powers, breaking the silence imposed on them in life. They "speak" with a most corporeal presence, and to effect.

Finally, my own professional interest as a cultural anthropologist inspired a selection that seemed to offer some insight into the Bengali world of the supernatural itself, the cultural beliefs and ideas that underlie the otherworldly entities who are the protagonists of the stories in this anthology. These entities are not the witches and vampires popular in Western literature and cinema – they draw from Bengali conceptions of power beyond the mundane and everyday world. They act upon the world of the living in their own, unique way.

In Bengali belief generally, several types of supernatural entities are traditionally included under the broad rubric of bhoot. Male supernatural entities include the brahmadaitya, the ghost of a brahman and, the purest caste among ghosts; the kandhakata, or headless ghost; the pechobhoot, who wanders around infants; the jakhbhoot, or a young boy buried alive in an underground vault filled with riches, so that his spirits may protect this wealth for legitimate successors; the harabhoot, who lives near ponds and drags unwary swimmers to their death by drowning them; the barulbhoot, the ghost that turns in the wind swirls of a hurricane during the Kalbaishakhi, the fierce thunderstorm of spring; and the nishibhoot, who calls people out at night to die of wandering.

Female entities include the pretini, colloquially, petni, which is the dissatisfied and often malevolent soul of the woman whose last rites were improperly performed; the pishachi, the eater of flesh and drinker of blood, who can fly and take human form; the dakini and yogini, a follower of the divinities Shiva, Kali or Durga, and who haunts cremation grounds. From dakini comes daini or witch, who is in fact a woman in the flesh, possessed of the "evil eye," with malevolent, life-destroying powers. Then there is the shankhachurni, colloquially, shakchunni, the soul of a woman who has died in the married state and longs to return to it.

In popular tradition, Bengali bhoots depending on who they are, live in desolate places – the forest, the lonely countryside, haunted houses or close to village ponds. So, brahmadaityas, favourites of the god Shiva, live in the woodapple, bel, tree, while shankhachurnis inhabit shaora shrubs and palm trees in rural areas. Contemporary stories, however, often place ghostly entities in the heart of Calcutta. Some bhoots may be as tall as two palm trees, others have arms that may be elongated at will. Still others are skeletal with hollows in the skull for eyes. Those bhoots who are fleshed out are usually dark of skin – though they may also be beautiful and seductive. Bhoots may be one-legged, or have feet that point backwards (a sure way to recognize a bhoot!). Some wear plain white cotton, others may be draped in a gamcha, a cotton towel. Shankhachurnis wear red-bordered white sarees, as married Bengali women do, have long, stork-like legs, flowing hair, and sprinkle cowdung mixed with water before them as they go, to purify the path on which they move. According to popular belief, a shakchunni can use her legs as firewood to keep a stove going, in lieu of the real thing, or stretch her arm to fetch an ingredient for the cooking pot from the next room. Some Bengali bhoots love fish! They trouble the living for fish, have a special predilection for charred fish, machhpora. In fact, they may break the necks of the living to get the fish they so desire. The special time of year for bhoots is the fourteenth day, chaturdashi, of the waning fortnight of the month of Kartik in October-November, the night of amabashya, that darkest night of the new moon.

In the stories in this anthology, some of the authors draw from the repertoire described so briefly and incompletely earlier. However, as works of creative imagination, the protagonists of these stories vary in appearance and in the expression of their powers, and the means by which they communicate their passion – their "stories" are, after all, different! As in any good work of fiction, the author weaves into his creation the rich strands of customs, folkways, religious beliefs and myths that make up her or his own cultural heritage. Like the "real" worlds of social relations, or politics, the world of the supernatural too constitutes its own reality, not to be sceptically judged by an increasingly "scientific" and "rational" mindset. To ask if witches and ghosts are "real" is to miss the point – to those who believe in them, they are most real. Every human culture, says the large body of work on the topic in cultural anthropology, has its own legions of supernatural entities, interacting with or intervening in – for better or for worse – the world of the living. Even that bastion of rationality, the West, has not dispensed with its hobgoblins, fairies, elves and ghosts. Witch covens are becoming increasingly popular, while there has been a recent resurgence of experiences with angels. The Madonna, in the meantime, continues over centuries to dispense her miracles to the true believer. For the Bengalis, then, priding themselves as they do on their rich literary and artistic traditions, on their erudition and sophistication, the supernatural is not to be dismissed as so much superstition. Such entities are integral, and unique, to the cultural world of the Bengali. It is probably a rare Bengali, growing up as a Bengali, who is unfamiliar with what a nishibhoot is, or a daini, a petni or a shakchunni! Again, what makes such entities endure in the cultural imagination are their very real connections with, in this context, women in the world of the living.

The stories in this anthology span more than a century and speak at different levels to the contemporary reader anywhere. For example, on the one hand, they speak universally of the pain of loss, of hungering after youth and beauty, or revenge for rape or betrayal, of greed. So, a long-dead woman communicates a snapshot of the pain of her unrequited love to a sympathetic housewife; a paralyzed woman, craving sexual pleasure, usurps the body of a young and nubile woman; the skeleton of a woman, greedy for gold in life, and murdered for it, haunts her husband; and a philandering husband, killed in an accident, saves his sharp-tongued widow from a con-man. Killed herself in the melee, she joins him in the skylight of their own home in eternal – and one assumes, contentious – reunion.

The stories speak too in the specific voice of a land, its people, their social groups (two of the stories highlight caste differences as integral to the plot), and beliefs. Where the fearsome and powerful, though protective, mother goddess Kali is widely worshipped, it is appropriate that the grievous outrage of a low caste woman raped and murdered by an upper caste man is avenged by the goddess herself – on behalf of all women thus wronged. The disembodied voice of a spinster aunt-turned-petni, calls by night (as nishibhoots do) for her beloved nephew, unable to sever her attachment – both to him and to the fish he used to bring for her in life. In a similar vein, a wife calls out forever by night to her husband, in eternal question about the wife he married upon her death. A mother fills the heavens, again eternally, with her cries of grief for a child murdered to protect a rapacious landlord's wealth. In a theme of rebirth and repetition, a seductive and shadowy woman lures, again and again, married men to their deaths. Another such entity evokes Bengal's Muslim past as she reveals the agony of her enslavement, driving men insane with her silent grief. The witch – the author based this story on a "real" witch he knew in rural Bengal – barren, widowed, of low caste and poor, vents her rage upon those who wrong her by drawing out their life force with her evil eye. And, in a very contemporary twist, those who rape the environment are avenged by entities of the forests who appear as seductive illusions, sometimes even as dogs, changing shape as they go, draining the blood from their victims or driving them insane.

Where social institutions silence the voices of so many of the protagonists of the stories in this anthology, it seems that in the minds of their creators – and therefore from within the culture – they find, powerfully, the means to break that silence. If not effectual in life, their special powers, in life or after death, affords (and not too ironically, since their end seems to be achieved!) them an agency, an ability to comment and act upon the world of the living from beyond the pale. The ghosts, witches and vampires of these tales are indeed as "real" as the Bengali women whose lives they draw from.

May, 2000   Suchitra Samanta

RABINDRANATH TAGORE

At Dead of Night

1

Doctor! Doctor!"

What a bother! Now, in the middle of the night – I looked around and saw our landlord Dakshinacharan babu. I got up quickly and pulling up the broken-backed couch, offered it to him, searching his face anxiously all the while. It was two thirty in the morning.

Dakshinacharan babu, his face devoid of colour, his eyes staring, said, "Tonight there is that same trouble again. And your medicine has not been of any use."

"Perhaps you are drinking too much again," I said hesitantly.

"That is a mistake you always make. It isn't drink. You will never be able to guess at the real reason behind my problems unless you hear out my account from beginning to end," Dakshinacharan babu said with great annoyance.

A kerosene lamp burnt weakly in a small tin box in a niche in the wall. I raised the wick. It became a little brighter, and let out thick smoke. Pulling up the pleats of my dhuti, I sat down on a packing case spread with newspapers. Dakshinacharan babu began to speak:

"It would be extremely difficult to find another housewife like my first wife. But I was young and full of life's vigour. I had also studied the theories of poetry very closely, and so was impatient with pure domesticity. I often thought of the couplet by Kalidasa that went:

> *Grhini sachivaha sakhi mithala*
> *priyasisya lalite kalabithau*

A wife may be instructed in the arts like a beloved student.

"But words of wisdom drawn from the arts did not impress my wife, and if I attempted to woo her with amatory talk of any kind, she would dismissively laugh it away. Just as god Indra's mount, the elephant Airabat, was harassed by the currents of the river Ganga, so excerpts from famous poems and expressions of romantic affection were washed away on the currents of her scorn. She had an amazing capacity to laugh.

"Then, some four years back, I fell into the grip of a dreadful disease. Racked with high fever, with carbuncles on my upper lip, I was near death. There was no hope that I would live. One day even the doctor gave up. Around this time, a relative of mine produced a holy man from somewhere who ground a root in ghee and then fed the mixture to me. Perhaps because of the medicine, or perhaps because I was destined to, I survived.

"During my illness my wife did not rest for even a moment, night or day. For all those days, this frail woman, using all her slender human reserves, fought unceasingly with Yama's messengers assembled at the door. With all her love, her heart, her care – she protected this undeserving life of mine as if sheltering with both hands an infant at her breast. Without food, without sleep ... she was oblivious to the goings-on in the rest of the world. Yama, the god of death, released me from his maw like a vanquished tiger and left. But lashed out at my wife as he departed, with grievous consequences.

"My wife was pregnant at the time, and some time later gave birth to a still-born child. Immediately after, she was beset by various ailments. Then, I began to look after her. She was embarrassed at this turn of events and exclaimed, Oh, what are you doing? What will people say?

At Dead Of Night

Do not keep moving in and out of my room day and night.

"At night, if I would try, surreptitiously, to fan her when she had fever while pretending to fan myself, she would try to snatch it away from me. If, because I was attending to her, my mealtime was delayed even by ten minutes, then that too would be an occasion for entreaties and censure. Even if I provided the smallest service, she would oppose me, saying, It isn't good for a man to go this far.

"I suppose you have seen our house in Baranagar. There is a garden in front of the house, and the river Ganga flows just opposite. Just below our bedroom to the south, my wife had fenced off a small piece of land with a henna hedge and had planted a garden of her own. In the entire garden, that little patch was the most simple and homely. In other words, here there was no riot of colours, overwhelming fragrance or fancy leaves overshadowing the flowers, nor were there proud little paper flags sporting Latin names flapping beside measly little vegetables in pots. Here the Chinese jasmine, the jessamine, the rose, the gardenia, the oleander and the tuberose grew in abundance. There was a white marble base around an enormous bakul tree. When she had been well, my wife would herself have this platform washed twice a day. During summer, when her work was done, this was where she would sit. She could see the Ganga from here, but the babus sailing on the river could not see her.

"One evening in the month of Chaitra¹, during the fortnight when the moon waxed, after being confined to her bed for many days, she said, I feel restless, lying closed up in this room. Today I'd like to go and sit in my garden.

---

¹ **Chaitra** is the last month of the Bengali calendar, from the middle of March to the middle of April.

"I helped her up tenderly and very slowly led her to the stone platform under the bakul tree and laid her down on it. I could have placed her head upon my knee but I knew that she would consider this abnormal behaviour, so I brought a pillow and placed it under her head.

"Fully blossomed bakul flowers drifted down upon us in ones and twos, and the moonlight sifting through the branches lay like filigree upon her thin face. It was peaceful and silent all around. In that fragrant and shadowy darkness, sitting in a corner, my eyes filled with tears as I looked at her.

"I moved up to her slowly and held a fevered and frail hand in both mine. She didn't object to this. After sitting for a while this way I said, I shall never forget your love.

"I realized immediately how fatuous my words sounded. My wife laughed out loud. That laugh! A little shy yet blissful with a little disbelief as also biting mockery. Without saying anything at all in protest, her laughter conveyed, It is not possible that you will never forget me, nor do I expect it of you.

"Fearing just this sweetly piquant laugh I had never had the courage to speak romantically to my wife. The thoughts that I entertained about her in her absence would, in her presence, seem downright trivial. Why those very words, which in print moved me to copious tears, when spoken aloud appeared so laughable, I do not understand to this day.

"One can debate in conversation, but there is no arguing with laughter, so I had to fall silent. The moonlight grew more luminous, and a cuckoo called restlessly. I sat and wondered how the female koel could remain unresponsive even on such a lovely moonlit night.

"Despite all the medical treatment, my wife's illness showed no sign of improving. The doctor said that it might help to give her a change of air. So I took my wife to Allahabad."

At this point Dakshina babu suddenly started, and broke off. He looked suspiciously at my face, and then, resting his head in his hands, appeared to be lost in thought. I too kept quiet. The light of the kerosene lamp flickered in its alcove and the hum of mosquitoes sounded clearly in the silent room. Suddenly breaking out of his silence, Dakshina babu resumed speaking:

"In Allahabad Doctor Haran attended to my wife's treatment. Finally, after no improvement in a long while, the doctor, as well as my wife and I, realized that her disease was incurable. She would be an invalid for life.

"One day my wife said to me, When this disease cannot be cured, and neither is there any chance of my dying soon from it, how long can you live with this vegetable? Get married again.

"These words were uttered matter-of-factly, as if they were the most logical and thoughtful things to say, with not the slightest hint that they were also profoundly courageous, noble and far from trivial.

"This time it was my turn to laugh. But did I have the same capacity to laugh as she did? I began, like the hero of a novel, to say loftily, As long as there is life in this body ...

"She stopped me and said, Come, come! No more. I have had enough of your speeches.

"Not admitting defeat, I said, In this lifetime I cannot love anyone else.

"My wife burst out laughing. And I had to restrain myself.

"I do not know whether I honestly admitted, at the time, even to myself, that this ceaseless caring for an invalid had made my heart weary — though I now realize this. I could not even imagine not looking after her. Yet, the thought that I would have to spend my entire life caring for a permanent invalid oppressed me. Alas, when in my youth, I had looked ahead, caught up in love's illusion, with the hope of bliss and deluded by her beauty, my entire future had seemed to blossom before me. But now, from this day on to the end, only a hopeless, vast and parched stretch of desert remained.

"She must have noticed this desperate weariness in all my care of her. I did not know then but am certain now that she could read me as easily as a child's primer. So, when I would act like the hero of a novel and hold forth dramatically, she would begin to laugh with deep affection and helpless amusement. She knew my deepest, unspoken, innermost thoughts. Even today, when I think of it, I feel like dying of shame.

"Doctor Haran belonged to our caste. I would often be invited to his house. After I had been going over for a while, he introduced me to his daughter. She was unmarried, and probably around fifteen years of age. The doctor said he had not yet found a suitable groom for her and so had not arranged for her marriage. But I had heard rumours – the girl's lineage was blemished.

"But she was not lacking in any other respect. She was as beautiful as she was educated. And so, once in a while, because I would spend time conversing with her on various subjects, it would be late by the time I came home, long after my wife should have had her medicine. She knew that I had gone to Doctor Haran's house but never asked me the reason for my delay.

"I began to see a mirage in the desert again. My thirst had reached its peak, and the sudden sight of clear water, full to the brim, made it impossible for me to drag my mind away from it.

"The room of the invalid grew doubly distasteful to me. It was then that I grew even more careless and lackadaisical about the daily nursing of my wife and giving her her medication on time.

"Doctor Haran would frequently remark to me that death is preferable for those suffering from incurable diseases since neither they themselves, nor those close to them, could ever be happy. While such general observations are innocent, perhaps he should not have raised the subject with reference to my wife. But doctors seem to be so insensitive to life and death, that they are quite unable to understand how others feel.

"One day I heard my wife telling Haran babu in the next room, Doctor, why are you making me swallow these useless medicines and increasing our bill at the dispensary? When my very existence is a disease, give me something to hasten its end.

"The doctor said, Don't say such things!

"I was deeply upset when I heard these words. After the doctor left I went to my wife's room, and sitting on the edge of her bed, slowly began to stroke her forehead. She said, This room is too hot, go outside. It is time for you to go for a walk. If you don't go out for a while, you will not feel hungry at night.

"To go out meant going to the doctor's house. I had myself told her that a walk would increase my appetite. I can now say with certainty that she knew my ploy. I was naive, and thought she was too."

Having said this, Dakshinacharan babu sat quietly for a long time with his head resting in his palms. Finally he said, "Please bring me a glass of water." After drinking the water he began again:

"One day the doctor's daughter, Manorama, expressed a desire to meet my wife. I do not know why, but I somehow did not like her request. However, I did not have a good reason to refuse her. One evening she arrived at our home ...

"That day my wife's pain had been more acute than usual. At such times she would be extremely still and silent. She would sometimes clench her fists and her face would turn blue, in mute expression of pain. The room was silent and I was sitting on the edge of her bed. Perhaps she did not feel up to asking me to take my daily constitutional, or perhaps she desired that I be near her when she was in such pain. The kerosene lamp had been placed by the door to keep the light from hurting her eyes. The room was dark and silent – a silence punctuated only by the sound of her sighs of relief each time a spasm of pain lessened in its intensity.

"Manorama came and stood at the door of the room. The light of the lamp fell upon her face from across the room. She hesitated at the door, unable at first to see clearly in the shadowy light.

"My wife started, and clasping my hand cried, Who is that! Terrified, in her weakened condition by the sight of a stranger, she repeated in a choked voice, Who is that? Who is that, dear?

"I do not know what foolishness possessed me, but I immediately said, I don't know who it is. As soon as I had spoken I felt as if I had been whiplashed. The next moment I hurriedly said, Oh, it's our doctor's daughter!

"My wife looked once at my face. I could not look at hers. Please come in, she invited in a weak voice after the briefest of pauses, and turning to me said, Hold up the light.

"Manorama came into the room and sat down. She and my wife engaged in polite conversation. Soon after, the doctor arrived.

"He had brought two bottles of medicine from his clinic. Showing these to my wife, he said, This blue bottle has a massage ointment, and this one is for you to drink. Take care, don't mix the bottles, this blue one contains poison.

"He cautioned me as well and placed the two bottles on a table next to the bed. Before leaving, he called his daughter.

"Manorama said, Baba, why don't I stay? There is no woman here, who will look after her?

"My wife grew agitated and said, No, no, don't trouble yourself. There is a maid who has been with us for a long time, she looks after me like a mother.

"The doctor laughed, She is the goddess Lakshmi herself. She has always looked after others, and cannot bear to be waited upon.

"The doctor and his daughter were preparing to leave, when my wife said, Doctor, my husband has been sitting in this closed room for a long time, perhaps you could take him out for a while.

"The doctor said to me, Do come along, we can take a walk by the river.

"I resisted a little but gave in quickly enough. Before he left, the doctor cautioned my wife once more about the two bottles of medicine.

"That night I had dinner at the doctor's house. It was late by the time I came home. I found my wife writhing in pain. Overcome by remorse I asked, Has your pain increased?

"She could not answer and looked silently at me. Her voice by then was completely choked.

"I called for the doctor at once even though it was so late at night.

"At first the doctor could not fathom what had happened. Finally he asked my wife, Has your pain increased? Perhaps you could be massaged with the medicine?

"He picked up the bottle, and found it empty.

"He asked my wife, Have you taken this medicine by mistake?

"My wife nodded, Yes.

"The doctor instantly got into his car and raced home to get a

stomach pump. I fell, half-conscious, upon my wife's bed.

"Then, as a mother comforts her ailing child, she pulled my head to her breast, and, with the touch of her hands, tried to tell me what was in her heart. Through her compassionate touch she told me again and again, Do not grieve. It is for the better, you will be happy, and knowing this I shall die happy myself.

"When the doctor returned, all of my wife's suffering had ceased, as had her life."

Dakshinacharan had some water yet again, and exclaimed, "Oh, it's so hot!" He quickly went outside and paced the veranda a few times, then came and sat down again. It was apparent to me that he did not want to speak. It was as if I had worked a spell to snatch his words from him. He began again:

"I married Manorama and returned home from Allahabad.

"Manorama married me with her father's consent. But when I spoke words of endearment and tried to win her heart with love, she remained unsmiling and reserved. How could I know what had upset her?

"About this time my desire to drink became very acute.

"One day, early on an autumn evening, Manorama and I were strolling in the gardens of our house in Baranagar. An eerie darkness had descended. We could not even hear the birds flapping their wings in their nests. All we could hear was the rustle of the tamarisk trees trembling in the breeze on both sides of the dark and shadowed path.

"Feeling tired, Manorama lay down on the white marble platform under the bakul tree, her head on her arms. I too came and sat beside her.

"The darkness seemed even more intense there. The little patch of sky that could be seen was dense with stars. The drone of the crickets beneath the trees seemed to have woven a slim border of sound trimming the vast silence beneath the endless expanse of sky.

"That evening too I had had some wine, and was feeling slightly unsteady. Once I had grown accustomed to the dark, the pale indistinct outlines of the tired reclining woman with her slackened anchal aroused in me an irresistible emotion. I felt she was a shadow, one whom I could never ever hold in my arms.

"Suddenly a fire seemed to break out at the top of the dark tamarisk trees. The thin yellow dying moon slowly climbed above the treetops into the sky. The moonlight fell upon the weary girl in her white saree, lying on the white marble. I could contain myself no longer. Coming close to her I caught her hand in both of mine and said, Manorama, you don't believe me, but I love you. I will never forget you.

"I started as I said this. I remembered how I had spoken exactly the same words, at some other time, to one other. And at that instant, rising above the bakul branches, above the tamarisk tops, under the waning yellow gibbous moon, from the east shore of the Ganga to the distant western banks – Ha-ha ... ha-ha ... ha-ha – a laugh glided swiftly past. I could not say whether it was a heart-rending laughter or a lament that rent the skies. I fell from the marble bench in a faint.

"When I regained consciousness I found myself lying on my bed in my room. My wife asked, Why did this suddenly happen to you?

"I shuddered and said, Did you not hear it, the laugh that filled the skies?

"My wife laughed and said, Was that a laugh? That was a huge flock of birds – we heard the sound of their wings. Are you so easily frightened?

"In the light of day I could accept that it was indeed the sound of birds in flight, it being the season when the swans flew down from the north to feed by the banks of the river. But as evening fell I could not keep this faith. Then I would perceive the darkness dense with laughter, seeking but an excuse to shatter the blackness and resound across the heavens. Finally it came to this – that as soon as evening fell, I would not have the courage to speak to Manorama.

"Then I left the Baranagar house and, with Manorama, set off on a voyage by boat. The river breeze in the month of Aghrayan blew away all my fears. For a few days I was most happy. Charmed by the scenic beauty all around, Manorama too appeared to slowly open the doors of her heart to me.

"Leaving the Ganga behind, and rowing past Khare, we finally arrived at the Padma river. The fearsome Padma lay like an emaciated female serpent, lifelessly hibernating in her pit during the season of hemanta. To the north lay desolate stretches of sand, with no sign of human habitation. And to the south, at a height, the village mango groves stood in trembling supplication at the mouth of this demon river. Every now and then, the Padma tossed this way and that in her sleep, and her banks, torn asunder, fell off in large chunks.

"Thinking this was a good place where we could go for walks, I anchored the boat.

"We went quite far one day as we strolled. As the golden shadows of the setting sun merged with the dusk, the pure light of the waxing moon became brighter. And when, on that endless stretch of white sand, wild unfettered vibrant moonbeams flooded the horizons, it seemed as if we were the only wanderers in the deserted dream-

---

Aghrayan is the eighth month of the Bengali calendar, from the middle of November to the middle of December.

kingdom of the moon. A red shawl covered Manorama's head, framed her face and enveloped her body. When the silence deepened and there remained only emptiness and a whiteness, limitless, eternal, Manorama put out her hand and clasped mine. Coming very close, she seemed to surrender to me her body and soul, her life and youth. With delighted heart I thought, how can one love greatly within the confines of a room? For where could two such people be accommodated but under this vast, open, boundless expanse of sky? Then I felt, we have no home, no threshold, nowhere to return, and hand in hand we would roam forever in this moonlit emptiness – no aim in mind, no path to follow.

"Wandering thus, we saw a little pool not far from us in the middle of that barren and sandy stretch. After the Padma had moved away, she had left behind some water, which now remained encircled by land.

"Upon that sand-surrounded stillness of water a shaft of moonlight lay as if in a swoon. We came up to this place and stood there – Manorama, thinking of something looked at me, and the shawl slipped off her head. I lifted her face, aglow in the moonlight and kissed her.

"At that moment, in that lonely uninhabited desert, a sombre voice called out, Who is that? Who is that? Who is that?

"I started, and my wife trembled. But we both realized immediately that this sound was neither human nor ghostly, but the call of the water birds. They had been startled by our sudden intrusion into their safe and solitary homes this late in the night.

"Disturbed by that sudden fright we quickly returned to the boat. At night we lay on our bed. Tired, Manorama soon fell asleep. Then, in the dark, someone stood near the mosquito net, pointed a long, thin skeletal finger at the sleeping Manorama and mumbled in my ear again and again, Who is that? Who is that? Who is that, dear?

"I quickly arose, struck a match and lit the lamp. At that instant the shadow melted away and shaking the mosquito net, rocking the boat and freezing the blood in my sweat-soaked body, a laugh – ha-ha ... ha-ha ... ha-ha – wafted away through the night. Over the Padma, over its banks, over the sleeping villages and cities beyond – as if it were floating away for ever and ever over distant lands, growing feebler and feebler as it floated away into infinity. It seemed as if it then left this world of life and death and gradually grew as tiny as a needlepoint. A sound so faint I had never heard and had not even imagined. As if there was an eternal sky inside my head and that cry, no matter how far it went, could not escape the confines of my skull. Finally, when this became more than I could bear, I thought that if I did not put out the light I would never be able to sleep. As I put out the light, again, near my mosquito net, at my ear, that choked voice whispered, Who is that? Who is that? Who is that, dear? And in rhythm with my heartbeat, it continued to reverberate, Who is that? Who is that? Who is that, dear? Who is that? Who is that? Who is that, dear? In that dark night, in the silent boat, my clock came to life and it too chimed out, Who is that? Who is that? Who is that, dear? Who is that? Who is that? Who is that, dear?"

As he spoke, Dakshina babu grew pale, and his voice strangled in his throat. I touched him and said, "Have some water." At that moment the flame of my kerosene lamp sputtered and went out. I suddenly saw it was light outside. Crows were calling. A magpie began to whistle. The creaking sounds of a bullock cart could be heard in front of my house. Then Dakshina babu's face changed

• AT DEAD OF NIGHT •

suddenly. There was no trace of fear in it. He was embarrassed at how much he had revealed, caught up in the imaginary fears and delusions of the night, and he grew very angry with me. He suddenly arose and without so much as a by-your-leave walked quickly away.

Again, at midnight the next day, came a knocking at my door, and the cry, "Doctor! Doctor!"

"Nishithe." From *Rabindra Rachanabali,* vol 10, Visva Bharati, 1396 BS.

RABINDRANATH TAGORE

The Hungering Stones 2

My cousin and I, having completed our travels around the country during the Puja holidays, were returning to Calcutta when we met the babu on the train. We mistakenly assumed, from his manner of dress, that he was a Mohammedan from western India. We were further intrigued by his conversation. He discoursed with such expertise on every subject under the sun that it seemed the Creator himself had first consulted him before beginning His work. That such unheard of profound and mysterious events lay beneath the everyday functioning of the world – that the Russians were so far advanced, that the English had such and such ulterior motive, that the Indian princes had worked themselves into a royal mess – having known none of this, we had been quite at peace with ourselves. Our new acquaintance gave a little laugh, and observed, "There happen more things in heaven and earth, Horatio, than are reported in your newspapers." This was the first time that we had left home and we were suitably awed by this man and his ways. He would, on the slightest pretext, launch on a discourse upon science, offer an interpretation of the Vedas, or quote a couplet from Persian poetry. Being quite ignorant about all three topics, our admiration for him grew steadily. Finally, my Theosophist cousin came to the firm conviction that our co-traveller must have some kind of connection with the supernatural – a wonderful magnetism or divine power, an astral body, or something of the sort. He was listening with perplexed yet rapt devotion to even the most ordinary utterances of this extraordinary man, and secretly taking notes. I felt from his manner that the extraordinary individual too realized this, and was quite flattered.

The train came to a halt at the junction and we assembled in the station waiting room for the next train to arrive. It was ten thirty at night when we learned that our train had been delayed because of some problem. I had just decided to unroll my bedding upon the table and go to sleep, when that extraordinary person embarked upon the story I write below. I could not get any sleep that night.

After a falling-out in matters of administrative policy, I left my job at Junagarh and started work with the Nizam of Hyderabad. Being at the time a young and strong man, I was appointed the collector for cotton duties at Barich.

Barich is a most delightful place. The river Susta, its name a corruption of the Sanskrit swachhatowa which means crystal clear, translucent water. Like a skilful and nimble dancer, it weaves its way along its pebbled and rocky bed, through extensive forests at the foot of desolate mountains. Along its steep banks, high above a hundred and fifty steps, stands a marble palace in solitary grandeur amidst the foothills. There is no habitation nearby. Barich village and its cotton market are quite some distance from there.

Nearly two hundred and fifty years ago, Shah Mahmood the Second had built this palace, in this lonely place, to indulge his pleasures. In his time, fountains of rose-scented water bubbled over in the baths, spraying the soft bare feet of lovely Persian maidens as they sat with open tresses upon cold marble thrones of stone, playing the sitar and singing ghazals about vineyards.

Now those fountains flow no more, there is no song, no fair feet tread lovingly upon the white stones. Now the house is the huge and empty habitation of a companionless tax-collector afflicted by solitude. However, Karim Khan, an elderly clerk at the office, had repeatedly warned me not to live there. He said, "If you like, stay there by day but do not spend the night." I had laughed off his fears. The servants informed me that they would work till evening, but would not stay the night. I said, "So be it." Even thieves feared the ill reputation of this palace and did not dare venture there.

At first the oppressive solitude of this deserted stone palace sat like a weight upon my heart. I would stay away as much as I could, work without rest, and return to fall into an exhausted sleep.

But before a week had gone by, the palace seemed to draw me into its spell, captivating me with some wondrous intoxicant. I cannot quite describe what came over me, nor can I make people believe what I felt. The house seemed to enwrap me in itself like some living organism, digesting me in its magical juices.

Perhaps this process had begun as soon as I had set foot in the house – but I remember that day, clearly, when I first became conscious of it.

It was the beginning of summer, and the market was dull. I had little work at hand. Just before sunset, I was sitting in an easy chair at the foot of the stairs by the bank of the river. The Susta had shrunk in size, its sandy banks on the other side glowed in the afternoon light. The pebbles glistened at the bottom of the clear and shallow water. No breeze disturbed the stillness. From the hills close by, a thick and delicious scent of wild basil, mint and aniseed filled the air.

When the sun sank behind the mountain peaks, a dark curtain descended upon the day's stage. Because the mountains screen the setting sun, twilight is short-lived in these parts. I was contemplating going for a quick canter on my horse when I heard the sound of footsteps on the stairs. I turned to look, but saw no one there.

As I turned back, thinking my senses had played a trick upon me, I heard the sound of several feet – as if many people were rushing down the stairs. My whole being thrilled with fear, and a wonderful exhilaration. Even though I could see no one, I had the distinct feeling that many young girls, intent on pleasure, were joyously descending the steps to bathe in the Susta's waters that summer evening. Even though there was not a sound that evening, at the foot of the silent mountains, on the banks of that river, in that deserted palace, I heard, like the hundred voices of a waterfall, the sweet, indistinct laughter of the girls as they ran past me, chasing each other down the stairs to bathe in the river. It was as if they did not see me at all. Just as they were invisible to me, I seemed invisible to them. The river was as calm as it had been earlier, but I now clearly felt that the slight currents in the shallow waters had been agitated by several braceleted hands – as if the girls were laughingly sprinkling each other with water, as if their splashing feet sent up sprays of foam, like fistfuls of pearls thrown up at the sky.

I could feel a trembling in my breast, though whether this was because of fear, or joy, or curiosity, I couldn't say. I wanted desperately to see them clearly, but there was nothing to see. I thought, perhaps if I listened carefully, I could hear what they said to each other – but my utmost efforts brought only the sound of crickets to my ear. It seemed as if an impenetrable curtain, two hundred and fifty years old, hung in front of me. I thought, if I carefully lifted up one corner of it, I would see an enormous assembly gathered there – but I could, in fact, see nothing in that thick darkness.

Suddenly a rush of breeze disturbed the stillness. The placid waters of the Susta rippled like the hair of heavenly nymphs and, in unison with the forest enveloped by the shadows of dusk, suddenly murmured and I awoke with a start, as from a nightmare. Call it a dream, or truth itself, a glimmer of the past had just danced before me like a mirage and disappeared in an instant. Those enchanting incorporeal creatures, who ran past me on lightning feet with soundless peals of laughter as they jumped into the Susta's waters, did not rise and return up the stairs squeezing water from their anchals. Just as the breeze carries away a fragrance, they seemed to disappear on a breath of spring.

I feared at the time that perhaps the Muse of poetry had taken advantage of my loneliness to settle upon my shoulders, come to cause the ruin of an unfortunate who makes a simple living by collecting duties on cotton. I thought I would have a good meal – an empty stomach is the source of all sorts of incurable diseases. I called my cook and commanded a spicily-fragrant, ghee-rich, Moghlai-like repast.

The following morning the whole affair appeared eminently laughable. In a happy frame of mind, donning a sola topee like an Englishman, I drove the tandem myself to work. Since I had my quarterly report to make that day, I expected to be home at a late hour. But as evening fell, something seemed to draw me ever more powerfully back to the house. Who it was I cannot say, but I felt that I could not be late. Everyone was waiting for me. I left the report unfinished, put my hat back on and clattered down the twilight-misted, tree-shaded lonely road, startling it to arrive at the dark and enormous palace that stood at the foot of the mountains.

The room facing the top of the staircase was especially large. Three rows of enormous columns supported an engraved and vaulting arched roof. Night and day this huge and vacant hall groaned under the weight of its own emptiness. When I reached, it was just before evening and the lamps had not yet been lit. As I pushed open the door and entered, it was as if I had let loose a complete pandemonium – as if some assembly scattered and fled pell-mell through the doors, and windows, and the veranda, in all directions. As I could see nothing, I stood there in utter amazement. I felt as if I were under a spell, so moved was I by emotion. The fragrant remnants of pomades and attars seemed to waft into my nostrils. Standing there in that dark and empty room, among its great columns of stone, I heard the sound of fountains splashing on marble. An unknown melody played on the sitar, the tinkle of gold ornaments, the music of anklets, the occasional sound of huge copper gongs marking the hour, far away the sound of the nahbat, the sporadic bell-like sounds of the chandeliers swaying in the breeze, the songs of the caged nightingales, the calls of pet cranes in the gardens – wove around me a melody from the world beyond.

I was caught up in an illusion. It seemed that this untouchable, inaccessible, unreal world was in fact real, all else was false, a mirage. In other words, the fact that I was I, Mr So-and-So, the eldest son of Mr So-and-So, an excise collector of cotton who earned four hundred and fifty rupees, who wore a sola topee and short coat and drove a tandem to work – appeared to me so immensely amusing and trivial that I stood in the centre of that huge, dark and silent room and burst into laughter.

At that moment my Muslim servant entered the room with a lighted kerosene lamp. Perhaps he thought that I had turned insane, but I remembered instantly that I was indeed Mr So-and-So, the eldest son

---

A **nahbat** is an orchestra in which the shehnai is the chief instrument. A nahbatkhana is the room or platform where the nahbat is played.

· The Hungering Stones ·

of the late Mr So-and-So. I contemplated too that only great poets could reveal whether in or beyond this world incorporeal fountains bubbled forth eternally and unseen fingers played timeless tunes on illusory sitars. But it was certainly true that I collected cotton duties at Barich and earned four hundred and fifty rupees every month. Then I thought of my earlier fantasies, and, sitting by the lamp-lit camp table with my newspaper, began to laugh at the jest my senses had played upon me.

Having read the newspaper, and eaten my Moghlai meal, I put out the lamp and lay down in a small corner room. Through an open window facing me, a distant but brilliant star from high above the dark, forested Arali mountains, seemed to observe Mr Tax Collector with single-minded attention. Bemused by these thoughts I did not know when I fell asleep. How long I slept I do not know either. Suddenly, I awoke with a start. It was not as if I had heard something in the room, nor had anyone entered it – for I could not see in the dark. The unblinking star above the dark mountains had since set, and the thin pale light of the waning moon now made a lustreless and diffident entrance through my window.

I could see no one at all. Yet it seemed to me that someone was pushing me gently. As soon as I was awake, she signalled, with a touch of her beringed fingers, that I follow her with great care. Even though there was no other living thing except myself in that many-chambered, empty, silent and echoing palace, I increasingly feared that someone might awaken. Most of the chambers in the palace were locked and I had never entered them.

Where I travelled that night, on silent feet, with bated breath, as I followed my unseen summoner, I cannot clearly recall today. How many narrow paths, how many long verandas, how many solemn, still and huge conference chambers, how many tiny, closed and secret rooms I traversed, I have lost count of.

Though I could not see my guide she was not imperceptible to my mind's eye. A Persian beauty, her firm, rounded marble-white arms showed through the loose sleeves of her robe. A fine veil fell from the edge of her cap over her face. A curved dagger hung at her waist.

It seemed to me that one of the one thousand and one nights of the Arab fable had come floating by. I felt, in that dark night, that I had travelled some narrow, dream-filled and unlit path in Baghdad; as if I had journeyed to keep some mysterious and dangerous tryst.

At long last my messenger stopped abruptly in front of a deep blue curtain and pointed down. I could see nothing there, yet my blood froze in my heart. I sensed that in front of that curtain, on the floor, clad in silk worked with gold brocade, sat a fearsome kafir eunuch, his legs spread apart, drowsing over an unsheathed sword upon his lap. My guide stepped lightly over his feet, and lifted up a corner of the curtain.

A portion of a Persian-carpeted room came into view. Someone sat upon a couch – I could not see who. All I could see were two delicate and lovely feet in brocaded slippers peeping out from beneath puffed-up, saffron-coloured pajamas, resting indolently upon a rose-hued velvet foot rest. On one side of the table was a bluish crystal fruit bowl full of apples, pears, oranges and clusters of grapes. Next to this stood two small goblets and a crystal carafe of golden wine, awaiting a guest. A wonderfully fragrant incense wafted from the room, so intoxicating that it nearly made me senseless.

As I, trembling in fear, attempted to step over the sprawled feet of the eunuch, he awoke with a start and his sword fell to the floor with a loud clatter.

The Hungering Stones

Suddenly hearing an awful scream I started, and found myself seated, my body drenched in perspiration, upon my camp cot. In the light of dawn, the waning, crescent moon had turned as pale as a sleepless invalid. And our crazy Meher Ali, in accordance with his daily morning ritual, was pacing the lonely path, shouting, "Keep away! Keep away!"

And thus my first night in an Arabian fairy tale came to a rather sudden end. However, a thousand more nights remained.

A severe discord developed between my days and my nights. I went to work each day, weary and exhausted, and cursed my dreamless, bewitched nights. And every evening my morning's work-bound reality seemed utterly insignificant, false and laughable.

After twilight I would be entangled, bewildered, in a web of intoxication. I would become some wondrous character in an unwritten ancient tale for which my Westernized short coat and close-fitting trousers would seem wholly inappropriate. I would instead dress with great care, and wear a red velvet fez upon my head, loose pajamas, an embroidered waistcoat, a long silk coat, and perfume a coloured handkerchief with attar. I would throw away my cigarette, and sit in a large and high-cushioned chair, smoking my rosewater-filled, many-coiled and enormous hookah, waiting in eager readiness for a most wonderful and romantic tryst that night.

And then, as the night grew increasingly dark, such remarkable events would transpire that I can hardly find words to describe them. It was as if fragments of an enchanting story, caught in a sudden flurry of spring breeze, were drifting through the strange rooms of this huge palace. They were visible only upto a point – the end was lost from sight. I would follow these whirling fragments from room to room all through the night.

In this whirling world of briefly glimpsed, disjointed dreams — here a hint of fragrant henna, there a stray note on a sitar, a sudden spray of perfumed water on a billow of wind — a heroine was seen as if in quick flashes of lightning. It was she who wore the saffron pajamas, she whose soft, rose-hued feet clad in upturned brocade slippers I had glimpsed, she who wore a close-fitting flowered brocade bodice worked with golden flowers, over her breast and a red cap on her head from which a golden fringe framed her fair cheeks.

She drove me to insanity. It was to see her that I waited in the infernal regions of sleep, for her that I wandered, room after room, the complex maze of pathways in that enchanted palace of dreams.

Some evenings, when I would be standing in front of the large mirror, lit by lamps on both sides, adorning myself like a shahzada, I would suddenly glimpse for a moment the reflection of the young Persian maiden, standing next to mine in the mirror. Swiftly arching her neck, and casting a sidelong glance, her large dark eyes and full crimson lips would suggest some deep unspoken yearning. Then, in a lithe and graceful dance-like movement she would twirl around, and in an instant, her grief, desire, bafflement, her amused arch glances, and a shimmer of ornaments like a shower of sparks from a fire, would merge into the mirror. A wild gust of wind, having robbed all the fragrances off the mountains, would burst in and blow out my lamps. I would leave my toilette and lie with closed eyes and thrilled body upon my bed. All around me, in the breeze, in the mingled aroma of the Arali mountains, abounding love and kisses and the touch of soft hands seemed to pervade that solitary darkness. I could hear sweet murmurs wafting by my ears, and a perfumed breath upon my forehead, while a soft-scented veil caressed my cheek again and again. It would seem as if little by little, a bewitching serpent would draw me into its intoxicating coils. I would sigh deeply, and numbed in body, would finally be overwhelmed by deep sleep.

One afternoon I decided to ride out on my horse – someone, I know not who, tried to stop me – but I did not listen that day. My English hat and short coat were hanging from a wooden rack. As I was gathering them, the sands of the Susta and the rustle of leaves on the Arali mountains signalled a disturbance. Suddenly a powerful whirlwind snatched my coat and hat upon its eddy and bore them away, as a sweet peal of laughter whirled on the gust of wind, striking scales of mirth, crescendoing until it mingled with the setting sun.

That day I did not go riding. And the very next day I put away that ludicrous short coat and English hat forever.

Again about midnight the same day, I sat up in bed and heard the sound of sobbing – soft, heart-rending cries, as if someone beneath my bed, beneath the floor, in a damp and dark tomb within the stone foundations of this enormous palace, was begging, "Save me, release me from this place! Break down the doors of cruel illusion, the depths of slumber, your futile dreams! Lift me upon your horse, hold me close to your heart, and through the forest, over the mountains and across the river, take me to your sunlit world! Release me, save me!"

Who was I! How could I save her? Was I capable of saving this deeply desirable beauty, drowning in a whirling, ever-changing dream-current? When did you exist, where did you exist, O eternal beauty! On the banks of which chill stream, in the shade of what orchard of date palms, to what wandering, homeless desert dweller were you born? Which Bedouin bandit plucked you from the vine like an unblown flower, and tearing you from your mother's lap, placed you upon his speedy charger, traversing the burning sands to deliver you to the slave market of some royal city? There, which emperor's emissary, observing your fresh bloom and shy loveliness, paid for you in gold and, putting you in a golden palanquin, took you across the seas and presented you at the chambers of his master? And, what a history they owned! Amidst the melodies of the sarangi, the tinkle of anklets, the emperor's golden wine, there was the glint of daggers, the hint of poison, the nuance of treachery! What boundless splendour, eternal imprisonment! Slave women on either side, their diamond bracelets glinting like lightning, pull at a large fan. The badshah lolls near the lovely bejewelled sandals beneath your fair feet. Outside, at the door, the Abyssinian, like Death's messenger, stands with unsheathed sword. And in that splendid flow of opulence, bloody, sinful, vicious, foaming with envy, fraught with intrigue, you, lovely blossom of the desert, were cast into what cruel death, tossed upon what savage precipice of power?

About then, the mad Meher Ali screamed out suddenly, "Keep away! Keep away! All's a lie! All's a lie!" I looked out and saw that it was morning. The peon handed me my letters and my cook salaamed and asked what he should prepare for me that day.

I felt that I could no longer live in that house. I collected my things and moved them to my office the same day. The elderly clerk, Karim Khan, laughed a little when he saw me. Irritated by his amusement, I made no comment and commenced my work.

As the day progressed towards evening I found myself becoming increasingly distracted – I kept feeling that I had to go somewhere at once, and assessing cotton appeared more and more trivial, the Nizam's royalty, too, began to seem an insignificant issue. The present, all that was around me, that walked, moved, worked, and ate, seemed petty, paltry and meaningless.

I flung my pen aside and closing my substantial account books,

The Hungering Stones

raced my tandem to the palace. I observed that my carriage stopped of its own accord at the instant of twilight near that stone edifice. I raced up the stairs and went inside.

Everything was still today. As if the dark rooms sulked in silence. My heart felt it would burst with penitence – but to whom should I confess, whom should I ask for forgiveness? Blankly I began to wander through the dark rooms. I wished that I could play on an instrument and break out in song to someone, Oh Fire! The moth which tried to flee from you has returned to die. Forgive him, burn his wings, reduce him to ashes!

Suddenly two teardrops fell from above on my forehead. Dark clouds had gathered over the Arali mountain peaks. The blackened forests and the Susta's inky waters waited as if in dreadful anticipation. The earth, the waters and the skies trembled all of a sudden. With snarling bolts of lightning a storm approached like a madman with snapped-off chains, screaming wildly as it burst through the huge dense pathless forest. The doors of the enormous rooms in the palace swung open violently, groaning agonizingly as they did so.

All my servants had remained at the office today and there was no one to light the lamps. In that clouded new moon night, in the pitch black dark, I got the distinct impression that a young woman was crouched over the carpet at the foot of the bed, tearing at her loosened hair with her hands, while blood streamed down her fair forehead, sometimes breaking out into harsh, dry laughter, sometimes heaving with sobs, tearing at her bodice with both hands and beating upon her naked bosom, as the wind roared through the open window and the pouring rain drenched her completely.

The storm raged ceaselessly through the night, as did her lament. In helpless grief I wandered from room to room. There was no one there. To whom should I offer solace? Whose dreadful outrage was this? From whence had this awful grief arisen? The insane scream sounded, "Keep away! Keep away! All's a lie!"

I saw that dawn had approached, and that even on such an unprepossessing day Mcher Ali, as was his wont, was walking around the house with his usual cry. It suddenly occurred to me that perhaps Meher Ali had lived in this palace once like myself. Though now no longer in its clutches, he had become insane, and unable to break away from the spell of this stone monster, was drawn to it every morning.

Then and there I ran upto him in the rain and asked, "Meher Ali, what lie do you speak of?"

Without replying, he pushed me aside, and like a wheeling bird transfixed by a python, began to go round and round the house, screaming as he went. As if in warning to himself, he shouted again and again, "Keep away, keep away, it's all a lie, it's all a lie!" I ran crazily through that dreadful storm to the office, and implored Karim Khan to reveal the meaning of it all.

The gist of what the old man said to me was this: Once, long ago, the palace had throbbed with turbulent storms of unfulfilled desires and intoxicated lust. Under the spell of these burning souls and unrequited passions, each stone was now starved and thirsting, and waited like a ravenous ogress to devour the living. Of all those who had spent three nights there, only Meher Ali had escaped their dreadful spell, although he had emerged insane. No one else had survived the palace's hungry maw.

I asked, "Is there no release for me?"

The old man replied, "There is a way, but it is most difficult. I will tell you what it is – but before I do, I must tell you the ancient story of a

Persian slave girl from that rose garden. Such an astonishing and heart-rending event has never occurred before in the history of the world."

At this moment the porters came in and announced that the train had arrived. So soon? By the time we had wrapped up our bedding, the train was at the station. An Englishman, just woken from sleep, was peering out of the window of a first class compartment, and attempting to read the name of the station. On spying our co-traveller he shouted out, "Hello!" and called him into his compartment. We climbed into a second class compartment. We did not learn who our friend was, nor did we get to hear how his story ended. I said, "That man found us naive, and had some fun at our expense – his story was concocted from beginning to end."

The argument that followed caused a lifelong breach between my Theosophist cousin and me.

"Khhudita Pashan." From *Rabindra Rachanabali*, vol 11, Visva Bharati, 1396 BS.

RABINDRANATH TAGORE
Manihara 3

My boat lay tied to the crumbling, decayed embankment by the river. The sun had already set.

The Muslim boatman kneeling at his prayers in his boat appeared etched in silhouette against the canvas of a blazing western sky. On the still waters of the river a million flecks of light changed, even as one watched, from pale to dark, from gold to rust, from one hue to another.

I could feel the tears rising in my dry eyes as I sat alone that evening, the chirp of crickets in my ears, on an embankment rudely cleft by the spreading roots of a peepul tree. Behind me stood an enormous decrepit mansion with broken windows, and a veranda that hung precariously from its supports. Suddenly, I started from head to foot as I heard a voice ask, "Where is the gentleman from?"

I saw a man so thin as if he were starved for food, as if the goddess of good fortune had determined to deprive him of her affections. He looked in fact like most Bengalis who, employed by foreigners, were long removed from their native culture. He wore a dirty, open-buttoned garment of coarse Assamese silk over his dhuti, as if he were only just on his way home from work. And when he should have been partaking of refreshments, the wretch was, instead, partaking of the evening breeze by the river.

The Bangla title **Manihara** (literally, mani meaning jewels, and in this story also the name of Phanibhushan's wife; hara meaning lost) also alludes to the Bangla saying "Mani hara Phani."

By **foreigners** the author refers to the British colonial rulers of India.

The newcomer sat next to me on the steps. I said, "I'm from Ranchi."
"What do you do?"
"I'm a businessman."
"What business?"
"Selling bundles of haritaki, silk and timber."
"What is your name?"
I paused briefly and came up with a name. But not my real one.

The man's curiosity remained unabated. "Why are you here?" he asked.

I replied, "I'm here for a change of air."

He seemed somewhat surprised, and observed, "Sir, I have been partaking of this air, and with it a daily dose of precisely fifteen grains of quinine for some six years now, and have yet to see any results."

"But one must admit, that compared to the air in Ranchi, there is quite a difference in this place," I countered.

He conceded, "Yes, of course, quite. Where do you intend to stay?"

I pointed to the decrepit house at the top of the embankment and said, "There."

I felt that he grew suspicious then, as if I had private knowledge of some hidden treasure in that dilapidated mansion. But he raised no further argument on this issue. However, he offered an elaborate account of the events that had transpired in this house some fifteen years ago.

He was a schoolmaster here. In his starving and disease-lean face, beneath a large bald head, a pair of enormous eyes burnt unnaturally bright in their sockets. He reminded me of the Ancient Mariner, that creation of the English poet Coleridge.

His prayers done, the boatman began to cook his meal. As the last

---

Haritaki, or Myrobalam, is a kind of fruit used medicinally and in rituals.

· Manihara ·

glow of the dying light faded away, the deserted dark mansion at the top of the embankment stood still and silent like an enormous phantom of its glorious past.

The schoolmaster began:

"Almost ten years before I came to this village, Phanibhushan Saha lived in this house. His paternal uncle Durgamohan Saha had no son. So Phanibhushan was the sole inheritor of his uncle's huge estate and business.

"But he was a victim of modernity. An educated man, he could walk into the Englishman's office in his shoes. He spoke English fluently. He even sported a beard, and thus seemed to have not even the remotest possibility of prospering under the English traders. One could see at once that he was a New Bengali.

"At home, too, he faced a problem. His wife was a beauty. On the one hand she had been to college, on the other she was a beauty, thus the old traditional ways were abided no more. So much so that if there was an illness, the assistant surgeon would be summoned. Their eating and dressing habits too followed this trend.

"You, sir, are probably married, so it will be pointless for me to observe that women like raw mangoes, hot chillies and a strict husband. The unfortunate husband who is cast off his wife's favours, suffers his fate not because he is ugly or poor, but because he is weak.

"If you ask me why things are this way, I will tell you that I have thought deeply about them. One cannot be at peace if one does not practise one's natural inclinations and abilities. The deer searches for the base of a hardwood tree to sharpen his horns, not the soft

---

Separate entities refers to Hindu genesis myths where the Creator was an undifferentiated Being from whom the universe, in its variety, including the two genders, arose.

stem of the banana plant. Ever since man and woman became separate entities, women have studied at length the wiles by which to subdue the unruly male. The husband who is subdued of his own volition leaves his poor wife with nothing to do – all those weapons sharpened through the ages and handed down by generations of grandmothers, those blazing arrows of fire, those serpent-coils – all come to nought!

"Women want to win love from their men by ensnaring them in their wiles, and if the husband is a simple soul who does not afford his wife that opportunity, his fate is a sorry one, that of his wife even more so.

"But bowing to the dictates of modern mores, man has not only lost his natural God-given lordly barbarism, he has also slackened the bonds that hold together the conjugal relationship. The unfortunate Phanibhushan too had imbibed these new fangled ideas and had emerged tamed – finding success neither in business nor in matrimony.

"His wife, Manimalika, obtained his love without effort, a Dhakai saree without tears, an armlet without pique. The woman in her, and her love, grew indifferent. She only took, and gave nothing. Her weak and guileless husband imagined that his giving would be enough to ensure her love for him. He had, of course, got quite the wrong idea.

"As a result of this she looked upon her husband as an instrument for getting her Dhakai sarees and armlets, this machine being so perfect that she never for a day needed to grease its wheels.

"Phanibhushan's hometown was in Phulbere, his place of business, here. He spent most of his time here pursuing his business. Though his mother was no longer alive, he had several aunts and other relatives who lived in the house in Phulbere. But it was for their welfare that

• Manihara •

Phanibhushan never took his lovely wife to visit them. He preferred to keep his wife to himself, and far away from the others in his household. However, it must be noted that, unlike other kinds of rights, keeping one's wife away from others and to oneself, does not guarantee exclusive rights over her.

"Manimalika was not particularly talkative, nor did she visit her neighbours much. Feeding a couple of Brahman priests on the occasion of a ritual, or giving alms to holy Vaisnavi women was not something that she would even consider doing. Nothing would ever be wasted because of her. Apart from her husband's affection, she hoarded everything with care. What did not cease to amaze was the fact that she had also preserved her remarkable and youthful loveliness, not spoiling even an iota of her beauty over the years. People said that even at twenty four Manimalika looked a fresh fourteen. Maybe those who have hearts of ice, who have never allowed themselves the burning agony of love, remain youthful forever, like misers who hoard themselves both inwardly and outwardly.

"Like a thick-leaved and fast growing vine, Manimalika, by divine decree, remained without fruit, unable to have a child. In other words, God did not give her that which she could understand and feel for, more than the jewels in her iron safe; that which, like the soft warmth of a spring morning, would melt her heart of ice and release upon her family a flood of affection.

"However, Manimalika was most efficient in her work. She would never keep too many servants. She could not bear to pay wages to someone for work that she herself could do. She had little thought for anyone else and loved no one but worked steadfastly and continued to hoard. And so she had little by way of illness, or grief, or anger, and presided over her amassed wealth in undisturbed peace and abundant health.

"For most husbands this would be enough. And why enough, almost rare. Only when the back hurts, does one recall its presence. Being reminded through agonizing love, each moment, twenty four hours of the day, that there is a wife within the protective folds of the household, is to suffer the backache of domesticity. While it is a matter of pride for a wife to show excessive devotion to her husband, it is not one of comfort for him, or at least that's my opinion.

"Sir, is it a man's share to calculate daily how much exactly he has of his wife's love, to weigh carefully everyday the fine differences, by how much he is short? Let my wife do her work, and I do mine, so we keep the balance at home. How much is said within the unsaid, what is not felt in what one other feels, what is merely hinted at in what seems apparent, what is large within the microscopic – God has not given such fine discriminations in love to men, He did not feel the need. But women sit down to weigh the tiniest bit of a man's caring, or lack thereof. They pick out and peck at the real motive behind his words, the real meaning behind his gestures to calculate the breeze that moves him, to turn his sails about, to point his boat in the right direction – because a man's love is a woman's strength, the wealth of her life. And this is why the Great Giver has placed the instrument of love inside the hearts of women and not around the hearts of men.

"But what God did not give men, they have begun to acquire for themselves. Poets have trumped over God and taken this invaluable instrument, and unthinkingly handed it over to the masses. I don't blame God for this. He had created men and women quite distinct from each other. However, civilization has not allowed us to maintain those differences. Now women are becoming more like men, and men like women. And so, peace and order have taken flight from home. Nowadays, not being sure whether one is being wedded to a man or a woman, the hearts of both the bride and the groom palpitate with dread!

"I can see you are growing irritated. I live alone, far from my wife. Distanced as I am from family life, many a profound truth comes to mind – these are not matters I may discuss with my students, I mention this to you in the course of the conversation, do think of it sometime.

"To sum it up, though there was never too little salt in the cooking, or too much lime in the paan, the betel leaf, Phanibhushan's heart felt an indefinable yet terrible turmoil. He found no fault with his wife, no shortcomings, yet he knew no joy. He would pour diamonds and pearls into her hollow cavern of a heart but they would end up in her iron safe instead, while her heart remained as empty as ever. His khura, Durgamohan, who did not understand the finer niceties of love, did not yearn for it so pathetically nor provide so generously, yet received abundantly his wife's affections. Keep in mind that it never pays to be a New Bengali in business and that, to be a husband, one has to be a man."

Just then the shrill yowling of foxes was heard from the shrubbery nearby.

This stopped the flow of the schoolmaster's story for a little while. It seemed as if the fun-loving fox community in that dark meeting ground was perhaps laughing out loud on hearing the schoolmaster's pronouncements on conjugal life, or his accounts of the hapless Phanibhushan. When their laughter died and the land and water seemed twice as silent, the schoolmaster rolled his blazing eyes in the darkness and continued his tale ...

"There suddenly came about a problem in Phanibhushan's

---

[1] **Khura** refers to one's younger paternal uncle.

complex and widespread business. What this was exactly, I, a non-business person, can neither understand nor explain. The substance of it was that he could no longer get credit on the market. If, even for five days, he could have, from somewhere, produced five hundred thousand rupees and quickly displayed it around the market, he might have been able to overcome the crisis and his business would have sailed smoothly forth.

"But he could not find that amount of money. He feared that even a rumour that he had gone to the local moneylenders to borrow money would affect his business adversely many times over. He would thus have to borrow from some source not familiar with him. There, however, he would need to have the appropriate mortgage.

"If jewellery is mortgaged, then the paperwork and delay is less, the work is accomplished faster.

"Phanibhushan approached his wife. But he could not do this as easily as a husband ought to be able to do. His love for his wife, unfortunately, was the sort of love the romantic hero of poetry would have for his lover, where one treads with caution, where all may not be revealed, like the lofty attraction of the earth and the sun, with an infinite distance in between.

"However, when the need arises, even the hero has to raise the issue of a bill of exchange, or of collateral, or of a document of purchase.

"But his voice choked, he tripped over his words — even in such a businesslike transaction, dull emotions and aching tremors intervened. The unfortunate Phanibhushan could not say, simply and clearly, My dear, I am in some trouble, please let me have your jewels.

"He did say it, but most timidly. When Manimalika, with a cold face, said neither Yes nor No, he was most grievously wounded, yet he did not strike back. Since he did not have in him an ounce of the machismo that so befits a man, where he should have taken her jewels by force, he even concealed from her his wounded feelings. He felt where only love has the right to enter, he would not let force trespass, even if it brought him ruin. Had he been chided for this, he would probably have made subtle arguments like – even if he no longer had credit in the market due to unjust reasons, he still had no right to loot that market. Similary, if his wife would not of her own volition give him her jewellery, then he could hardly take it from her by force. As credit in the market, so love at home – force was only for the battlefield. Has the Great Creator made a man so generous, so strong, so fine of stature, only so that he may argue with such fine precision? Does he have the leisure to sit about thus, exercising his refined mental faculties, or does that become him?

"Anyway, because of his idealistic and proud heart, Phanibhushan did not touch his wife's jewels and, hoping to raise money by other means, left for Calcutta.

"Usually a wife knows her husband much better than he knows her. However, if the husband is of a more complex nature, then even his wife's probing eye may miss some of it. Manimalika did not quite understand our Phanibhushan. The modern man lies beyond the pale of the intuitive competence of women, long established over tradition. Such men are unique. They have become as mysterious as women. The ordinary categories of men – namely those that are barbarians, or obtuse, or even the unseeing – cannot accommodate the modern man.

"So Manimalika turned for advice to a distant cousin from her village who used to work as the steward's subordinate in Phanibhushan's office. He did not have the temperament to rise in his line of work, but would seize any opportunity to obtain, on the basis of his kinship, his wages, and things over and above his wages. Manimalika called him, told him everything and inquired, Now what would you advise?

"He nodded his head like a wise man – to suggest that the matters appeared to bode ill. Wise men never seem to find the going good. He observed, Babu will never be able to get enough money, and then he will make demands on you for your jewellery.

"From what Manimalika knew of people, she understood that this was possible, and even probable. Her concerns intensified. She had no child. She had a husband of course, but she did not feel his presence in her heart – and so, that which was her only wealth, grew every year like a child. It was more than a metaphor. It was, in fact, Gold – to be worn on her bosom, around her neck, on her head.

"Manimalika grew cold at the thought that the precious ornaments that she had so lovingly hoarded for so long could, in a moment, be lost in the bottomless abyss of her husband's business demands. She asked, What is to be done? Madhusudan replied, Let us take your jewels and leave immediately for your father's house. The cunning Madhusudan silently determined how he could get a portion of those jewels, maybe even most of them.

"Manimalika agreed immediately.

"In the evening of the monsoon month of Ashar, a boat pulled up at this very embankment. On a clouded morning in dense darkness, to the ceaseless croaking of frogs, Manimalika, covered from head to foot in a thick shawl, climbed into the boat. Madhusudan, waking up from where he lay in the boat, said, Give me the box of jewels. Mani said, I'll give it to you later – now untie the boat.

Ashar is the third month of the Bengali calendar, from the middle of June to the middle of July.

"The boat was untied, and it sailed away swiftly on the powerful current.

"Manimalika had spent all night adorning herself with her jewels, each one, leaving no space uncovered from head to toe. If she put her jewels in the box they might get lost, she feared. But if she wore them, no one, short of murdering her, would be able to take them from her.

"Not seeing a box with her, Madhusudan was at first confused. He had not suspected that she had concealed her ornaments, more precious than her body and her soul, under her heavy shawl. Manimalika might not have understood Phanibhushan, but she had little doubt about Madhusudan's intentions.

"Madhusudan left a note with the steward stating that he was escorting the lady to her father's house. This steward had been in employ since Phanibhushan's father's time. Extremely annoyed, he wrote an irate letter to his employer, forgetting to dot his 'i's and cross his 't's, to the effect that a husband ought not to overly indulge his wife. The language was not very refined but the opinion was stated strongly indeed.

"Phanibhushan understood clearly why Manimalika had acted this way. What pained him most was that, even after he had refused to sacrifice her jewellery despite his desperate need for it, and had tried to raise the money with every means at his disposal, she had still suspected him of the worst; that even after all these years she did not know him at all.

"Where he should have been furious at the wrong done to him, Phanibhushan was merely wounded. The Creator has given man the right to punish; has put His thunderbolt in his hands. But if he still

---

Sraban is the fourth month of the Bengali calendar, from the middle of July to the middle of August.

cannot burst into flames in the face of wrongdoing to himself or to others, then fie on him! A man should, at small annoyances, flare like a forest fire, and women should, like the monsoon clouds in Sraban, shed tears for no reason – or so the Creator had ordained. But this is not so any more.

"Thinking about his wife's wrongdoing, Phanibhushan said to her in his mind, If this is what you have decided, let it be, I myself shall continue to do my duty. Phanibhushan, who should have been born some five or six hundred years into the future, when only spiritual powers will rule the world, had instead been born much before his time in the nineteenth century. And this Phanibhushan of the future had landed up in the nineteenth century and married a wife of an ancient age – one whose temperament the texts describe as destructive. He did not write a single letter to his wife, and decided that he would never discuss this matter with her again. What dreadful punishment!

"About ten days later, having gathered together the requisite funds to help him make up for his losses, Phanibhushan returned home. He expected Manimalika to have returned after entrusting her jewels to her father. He was determined to cast off his role of a seeker-of-favours of the previous day and approach her as a successful man-of-work. How ashamed she would be, how penitent at her refusal of him. Imagining such a scenario Phanibhushan walked up to the door of their bedroom in the interior of the house.

"He noticed that the door was closed. He broke the lock and entered the room, and found it empty. In a corner the iron safe stood open, with no sign of the jewellery. He felt a sharp pang in his heart. Life seemed utterly without purpose, and love and work without meaning. We lay down our lives at every inch of our life's cage, but there is no bird inside, nor will it ever stay if kept there. What is it, then, that we adorn each day with the jewels of our hearts' blood, the pearl strings of our teardrops? Phanibhushan kicked this cage aside which, though wrapped with his life, was still void.

"He did not want to make any effort to contact Manimalika thinking that she would return if she wanted to. The old Brahman steward came to him and said, What use is it to keep silent, we need to find out where she is. He then sent a man to Manimalika's father's house. The man returned with the news that Mani and Madhu had not arrived there yet.

"A search was instituted immediately. Men ran along the riverbanks, asking questions. The police were also asked to search for Madhu but there was no trace of anything – which boat they had taken, who their boatman was, what path they had taken ... nothing came to light.

"One evening, having lost all hope, Phanibhushan entered his deserted bedroom. It was the festival of Janmashtami that day. It had been raining unceasingly since morning. As usual a fair had been set up at the edge of the village for the occasion, and he could hear the first strains of the beginning of a jatra performance. The sound of torrential rain muted the notes of the players' songs. Phanibhushan sat alone by the portico door that swung loosely on its hinges, paying no heed to the stormy wind, the gusts of rain that came into the room, and the players' songs that drifted into his ears. An "art-studio" rendition of the goddesses Lakshmi and Saraswati hung on the wall of the room. On the clothes rack hung a thin cotton gamchha and towel. Two sarees, one with a narrow border and the other with stripes, were also hanging, pleated and ready, on the rack. On the tea table in the corner of the room stood a brass box with a few dried-up paans made by Manimalika herself. In the glass cupboard, her childhood collection of china dolls, bottles of perfume, a decanter of coloured glass, special cards, large cowrie shells from the sea, even empty soapboxes arranged in careful order. Her favourite tiny, spherical kerosene lamp, that she would light and place in the niche in the wall, stood unlit and dismal, the final witness to Manimalika's last moments there.

"Even she who departs, leaving everything bare behind her, leaves so many signs, so much history, so much of her lively self, her careful touch! Come Manimalika, come and light your lamp, light up your room, stand in front of the mirror and put on your saree with careful pleats. All your possessions are waiting for you. No one expects anything from you, only that you return, and with your eternal youth, your unblemished beauty, spread your glory on all these scattered, orphaned things and with your life yoke them together and infuse them with life in turn. These inanimate things cry out mutely, making this very house a cremation ground!

"Sometime deep into the night the sound of falling rain and the songs of the players had stopped. Phanibhushan remained sitting at the window. The darkness outside the portico was so all-pervasive, impervious, so intensely black, that it appeared to him to rise like the sky-piercing gateway to Yama's enormous mansion. Yet, if one cried at this gate, what has been lost forever might, for an instant, become visible. Then, perhaps, on this inky black canvas, on these cruel stones, one ray of that lost gold might glint again.

"Just then, a sound of knocking and the jangling of jewels reached Phanibhushan's ears. It sounded exactly as if someone were climbing the stairs of the embankment from the river's edge. The night and the dark waters of the river had merged and were indistinguishable from each other. Thrilling to the sound, Phanibhushan stared into the blackness as if he would tear at it with his eyes. His hope-swelled heart, his eager and pleading gaze became distressed. He could see nothing. The more determined he was to see what was out there, the more shadowed the world became. Nature, suddenly seeing a multitude of guests at the dead of night, seemed to draw yet another curtain with a swift hand across the cavernous entrance to her house of death.

"The sound approached gradually from the uppermost stair of the embankment, stopping in front of the house. The guard had closed the front gates and gone off to listen to the players. A hard knocking and jangling sounded on the closed gates, as if, along with the tinkle of jewellery, something very hard was pounding on them. Phanibhushan could bear it no longer – he ran across the unlit rooms and down the darkened stairway till he came to the gates which the guard had locked from the outside. The noise he made frenziedly shaking the gates brought him to his senses and he found that he had walked downstairs in his sleep. He was drenched in sweat, his limbs cold as ice, his heart beating unevenly, like a flickering lamp about to die out. Awaking from his dream he heard nothing more outside, only the sound of the monsoon rains mingled with the distant sound of the players singing the notes of dawn.

"Even though a dream, it had seemed so substantial, so close, that Phanibhushan felt as if he had missed by a hair the amazing realization of his improbable desire. The sound of falling rain, the distant strains of the raga Bhairavi, appeared to be saying to him, this waking is a dream, the world itself an illusion.

"There was a performance the next day too, and the guards had the day off. Phanibhushan ordered them to leave the gates open all night. The guard cautioned, Different kinds of people from various places are here for the fair, I am afraid to leave the doors open. Phanibhushan disagreed. The man argued, Then I will stay back and guard the house all night. Phanibhushan replied, No, you have to go and see the play. The guard was surprised at his insistence.

"The next evening Phanibhushan put out the lamp and sat down again on the veranda outside his bedroom. Though the sky was heavy with clouds, the rain had abated, and silence lay heavy as if in suspenseful anticipation of something undefined, something imminent. The tireless croaking of the frogs and the high pitched songs of the players could not penetrate this stillness, at best lending a certain peculiar incongruity to it.

"Sometime late into the night the frogs, and the crickets and the players fell silent, and another layer of darkness seemed to descend upon the already black night. The time, it seemed, had come.

"As on the day before, a hard knocking and a jangling sounded on the steps of the embankment. But Phanibhushan did not turn around for fear that his restless desire, his grasping efforts, would defeat all his desires, all his efforts, lest in his earnestness his emotional agitation blur his perception. He tried to subdue his perturbed mind and sat silent and immobile, like a wooden statue.

"Today, the tinkling sound came up the steps and entered the open gates. It went into the inner chambers, climbing the circular staircase to the floor above. Phanibhushan, breathless, his chest heaving like a boat in a storm, could barely hold himself back. The sound came from off the stairs, moving increasingly closer to the room. Finally the knocking and jangling came to a halt in front of the bedroom, but did not cross the threshold.

"Phanibhushan could sit still no longer. His suppressed desire burst forth in joy as he leapt like lightning from the couch and screamed, Mani! At once he awoke to see that his scream had shaken even the drapes on the windows of the room. And outside, as ever, the incessant croaking of frogs and the harsh singing of the players.

"Phanibhushan struck his forehead with force.

"The fair was over the following day. The shopkeepers and the players left. Phanibhushan ordered that no one but himself would stay in the house that day. The servants concluded that their master was probably performing some esoteric Tantrik rites. Phanibhushan fasted all day.

"That evening he sat by the window of the deserted house. There were patches of clear sky, and the stars twinkled brilliantly through the fresh wafting breeze. It would be a while for the waning moon to rise. Since the fair was now over, there were few boats on the brimming river and the festival-weary village lay in deep sleep after two days and nights of merrymaking.

"Phanibhushan sat on a couch, and leaned back to look at the stars. He remembered how when he was nineteen years old studying in a college in Calcutta, he would, of an evening, lie on the grassy banks of the Goldighi pond and look up at the stars. He remembered the glowing face of the fourteen year old Mani in his in-laws' home by the river, and how exquisitely painful that separation used to be, how the twinkling of the stars would keep pace with the beating of his young heart to the rhythms of spring! Today those same stars appeared to blaze across the firmament Mahmudgar's poetic observation on how very strange the world is!

"The stars faded even as he watched. A darkness descending from the sky, and a darkness rising from the earth met like eyelids and closed. Today Phanibhushan's heart had grown calm. He knew with certainty that today his desire would be fulfilled, that death would reveal its mysteries to he who waited so steadfastly.

"Like the night before, the sound arose from the river, and came up the stairs of the embankment. Phanibhushan, his eyes closed, and mind firmly in check, sat as if in meditation. The sound crossed the guardless gates and entering the inner chambers of the house began to climb, round and round the circular staircase, across the wide veranda, stopping for a while as it came to the door of the bedroom.

"Phanibhushan's heart beat agitatedly, his skin prickled – but today he did not open his eyes. The sound crossed the threshold and entered the room. Where the saree lay pleated on the rack, where the lamp stood in its niche, where the box with dry paan lay upon the tea table, and near the cupboard with its strange collection of things – the sound paused at every step, finally stopping by Phanibhushan.

"He slowly opened his eyes and saw that the light of the newly-risen moon, the tenth day of the lunar phase, had come into the room, and directly in front of his couch stood a skeleton. It had a ring on each of its eight fingers, bejewelled palms, bracelets on its wrists, armlets on its arms, a necklace around its neck, a tiara on its skull, every bone on its body sparkling with gold and diamonds. The ornaments were loose, hanging limply, yet not falling off the skeleton. Most fearsome, the eyes in the skull shone as if alive. Those same dark stars, that deep gaze, that brilliance, that same hard, still gaze. Eighteen years ago in a brightly lit living room, as the raga Shahana played, Phanibhushan had first seen those lovely, black and limpid eyes when he was being wed. Tonight, on this midnight in the month of Sraban, on the tenth day of the lunar phase, those eyes now froze the blood within his body. He tried desperately to close his eyes, but could not. With eyes like those of the dead, he stared unblinking at the apparition.

"Then the skeleton, staring fixedly at the stupefied Phanibhushan, raised its right arm and silently called to him with a finger. The diamond rings on its four fingers flashed blindingly.

"Phanibhushan arose silently, as if under a spell. The skeleton walked towards the front door. The clicking of bone and the jangle of ornaments mingled as it walked. Phanibhushan, like a mesmerized toy, followed. They crossed the veranda, and climbed down the circular staircase, to the sound of bones and jewellery. Crossing the veranda downstairs they entered the lampless, guardless gateway. Finally, crossing the gateway, they came upon the tiled pathway in the garden outside. The tiles sounded loudly at the knock of the bones. The meagre moonlight found no entrance through the dense and leafy branches to light their way. Through the heavy fragrance of the monsoon night, they walked along the shadowed path, finally coming to a halt at the top of the embankment.

"The bejewelled skeleton now climbed stiffly down the stairs it had ascended earlier, step by rigid step. The moonlight glistened on the strong currents of the monsoon-heavy river.

"The skeleton descended into the river and Phanibhushan followed. As soon as he touched the water, Phanibhushan's spell broke. He could not see anyone in front, only the motionless trees along the banks and the gibbous moon above, staring in silent amazement. Trembling from head to foot Phanibhushan stumbled into the current. Though he knew how to swim, his senses refused to obey him, and in that dream's brief awakening Phanibhushan sank to the fathomless depths below."

The schoolmaster, his story complete, was silent for a while. Suddenly he realized that but for the sound of his own voice, everything else around had fallen silent and still. For a long time I too said nothing, and he could not read my expression in the dark.

He asked, "Did you not believe this story?"

I asked him, "Do you believe it?"

He replied, "No. I will tell you a few reasons for this. First, Mother Nature is not a writer of fiction, she has plenty of other things to do ..."

I said, "And secondly, I am Phanibhushan Saha."

The schoolmaster seemed quite unabashed and said, "Then I had guessed correctly. What was your wife's name?"

I replied, "Nrityakali."

"Manihara." From *Rabindra Rachanabali*, vol 11, Visva Bharati, 1396 BS.

PRAMATHA CHAUDHURI

Sacrifice by Fire 4

European civilization has not yet penetrated the heart of my home; that is, the railroad has skirted off my village from afar. Therefore, even now, when we go home from Calcutta, we have to use the old modes of travel for some part of the route: boats during the monsoon and the palanquin during winter and summer.

The route by land and the one by water move in opposite directions. I had always used the boat to travel to and from home, and therefore, had not been familiar with the land route for a long time. And then, in July of the year that I passed my BA examinations, I was required to go home on some urgent work – but by land. I shall acquaint you today with the extraordinary events that occurred on this journey.

When I disembarked from the six o'clock train in the morning, I found that the palki bearers were waiting for me at the station. I cannot say that I was enthused about entering the palki upon seeing it. Assessing its dimensions with my eyes, I realized that it was about two feet in width, and less than four feet in length. I was also taken aback by the appearance of the bearers. Such skeletal human beings are probably never seen outside hospitals in other countries. Almost all had ribcages that poked out, with arm and leg muscles that had become rope-like. The first thing that caught my eye was that one part of their bodies – the stomach – was unusually taut and distended. Even though I am not a doctor, I guessed that inside their abdomens, their spleens and livers were growing apace. I remembered reading in the Brihadaranyak Upanishad that the sacrificial horse of the Ashvamedha ceremony had a liver and lungs the size of a mountain. For the first time I had found manifest proof that such comparison was not far-fetched.

I also felt shamed by the undeniable evidence that man's body could be so graceless, so decimated. Such a body seemed to openly offend human dignity. And yet, in our villages, Hindu courage survives by seeking refuge in just such bodies. They are Hindu despite being untouchables, and heroic, even though weak in body. They are hunters by caste. They kill boars with their spears, and traverse the forests to flush out the tiger – all done of course, to satisfy the stomachs. Compared to them, my handsome companion, the Bhojpuri darwan, looked quite princely in his red turban and white coat.

At first I felt most reluctant to ride a distance of twenty miles on the shoulders of these emaciated creatures. It would be excessively cruel, I felt, to burden my weight on these sickly, half-dead unfortunates.

Seeing me hesitate, the Muslim who had come from my house to escort me, laughed – "Master, climb in, you'll have no trouble. If you delay further, you will not be able to get home before four in the evening."

I cannot say at all that my enthusiasm to ride the palki increased upon learning that it would take ten hours to travel a distance of twenty miles. Still, since I had no alternative, I called on the goddess Durga for protection and crawled into that packing case. Obviously, I had by now convinced myself that being borne on the shoulders of men was not a sin. After all, we the rich people of the world, journey through our lives on the shoulders' of the poor. Besides, "political economy" has always maintained that a few rich and countless poor always have been, are, and always will be, the natural order of things. How many mantras we have learnt to lay our conscience to rest!

• Sacrifice By Fire •

Then, the palki began to move.

My escort had reassured me that his Master would not suffer on this journey. But it did not take me long to realize that his assurance was in fact only a consolation, proffered because his master's healthy body had never before been this disturbed. My futile attempts to pare my body's volume to that of the palki so agitated me, I cannot call the contortionist postures I adopted either lying down, or sitting up. If, for the Shalagram, both lying down and sitting up are the same, they are not so for humans. Thus, I had to labour ceaselessly to assume any one of these to my satisfaction. It was well nigh impossible not to spoil the crease of my dhuti and give up a veerasan position and move into padmasan. Yet I was forced to change positions every minute. I believe, that under these conditions, even one advanced in the discipline of yoga would not have been able to hold any one posture. Whenever I straightened my back, the roof of the palki violently struck the top of my head. As a result, like a new bride in the presence of her elders, I had to bow my back and keep my head demurely bent. Never before had I had the occasion to concentrate so long upon my navel but alas, due to a woeful lack of mental discipline, I could not compel my perturbed mind to focus on it.

However, I was not intimidated by this chaotic condition of my body. I was young then. My body had not yet lost its resilience. Actually, to tell you the truth, I was entertained to see the involuntary contortions my body was going through. I was wonderfully elated

---

Shalagram is a rounded black stone worshipped as the symbol of Vishnu.

The character is presumably referring to one of the six chakras in the human body on which the yogis concentrate and meditate. Nabhipadma, the lotus shaped chakra called the Manipur Wheel, is situated next to the spine on the opposite side of the **navel**.

as I felt the joyous caress of the gentle easterly breeze and gazed upon the lovely morning light. With the day's new awakening, my eyes and mind came alive and I was transfixed by the scenery. All around me the fields stretched endlessly. There were no houses, trees, shrubs, nothing – only fields, infinite fields – all of a level, and featureless, as boundless and vacant as the sky. Emerging from the stone-and-wooden pigeon-coops of Calcutta, my soul began to revel in the freedom of Nature's boundless generosity. All worries fell from me, and my mind became as unaffected and blissful as the sky – and like it, flushed gently with a joyous red lustre. Alas, this happiness was short-lived, because as the day progressed, the sun grew hot, as if Nature lay in a fever, and the temperature gradually rose to a 105 degrees. At about nine in the morning, I found that I could look outside no longer, the dazzle so seared my eyes. Hungering for some touch of green, my eyes searched the distance and met only with one or two acacia trees here and there. Needless to say, this did not quench the thirst of my gaze, because, whatever other virtues these trees might have, they have no verdant loveliness, no dark shade at their base. Slowly, within this treeless, leafless, shadeless, brilliant world and the cloudless sun-afflicted sky, a huge image of complete exhaustion emerged. Nature's monotonous face became unbearable to me. I opened a book and tried to read. I had brought Meredith's *Egoist* with me and had yet to read its final chapter. Having read some few pages at a stretch, I saw that the final chapter had become the first – that is, not one syllable had entered my head. I realized that the violent movement of the palki had quite confused my head. I shut my book, and requested the bearers to pick up the pace a little, promising extra money as incentive. This ploy proved to be successful. At ten thirty we had already arrived at the village where we were to break journey, that is, some half-hour before the scheduled time.

I cannot quite say that this village provided a charming and pleasant instance of an oasis in this desert. It had a small pond in the centre and on its three raised and levelled edges some ten or twelve straw huts, and a fig tree. Lowering the palki beneath this tree, the bearers ran to the pond, dipped themselves in it, sat down and began, still in their wet clothes, to eat a repast of yoghurt and dry, flattened rice. Seeing the palki the village wives appeared gradually to line up in a row on the banks of the pond. It is difficult to wax poetic about these women because, whatever their other virtues, they were neither beautiful nor young. Even if any of them had possessed a modicum of beauty it was lost in their dark skin, if a vestige of youth, it was concealed in their soiled and worn out clothes. Their clothes were so filthy that if pinched, they would have yielded a lump of dirt. What caught my eye was the silver jewellery which they wore on their arms and ankles. I noticed a pair of bracelets with the kind of exquisite craftsmanship that is not to be found in modern designs. It proved to me that though the lower caste Bengali women were not beautiful, the men of that caste did not lack an artistic temperament.

A half-hour later we resumed our journey. The palki began to travel at a leisurely speed because, after their meal, my carriers had become as sluggish as pregnant women. In the meantime, my body, mind, senses, the very essence of my being, had grown so exhausted that I shut my eyes and attempted to sleep. Gradually, I began to doze in the heat of the July sun and the pleasant swaying of the palki. But this was not just any drowsy state. Just as my body had assumed a position somewhere between being prone and sitting upright, my mind too floated between sleep and awakening. Nearly two hours passed in this condition. Suddenly a tremendous jolt woke me up – such a jolt that my spirit seemed to shoot up through my spine to the cranium! Starting awake, I saw that the matter was nothing more than this – that having deposited me with some violence beneath a banyan tree, the bearers had disappeared! When I asked their leader for a reason, he informed me that they had gone off to smoke some tobacco. This place, for the first time since I had begun my journey, impressed me with its loveliness. That banyan was in itself a hundred trees; on all sides myriad roots descended from it. Moreover, its leaves were so dense that the sun could barely penetrate its thick foliage. As if Nature had lovingly constructed this resting house of a thousand pillars for the weary and heat-afflicted traveller with her own hands. The shadows there were so dark that I mistook the time for twilight, but on opening my watch, I saw that it was but one in the afternoon.

I used this chance to extricate myself, with some difficulty, from the palki and to stretch my limbs. It took some fifteen minutes to get myself upright. Because, while my limbs had become quite cramped, the other parts of my body were absolutely numb. Some parts had begun to tingle, others were paralyzed, and yet others in a state of rictus. Once my body began to feel better, I thought of easing my muscles by walking around the huge tree. Having gone a little way, I saw the bearers assembled around their leader, Pandeji. I feared at first that they were conspiring against me, since they were all talking excitedly at once. But I soon realized that some other reason lay behind all this shouting and cacophony. I realized that what these men had been smoking was not tobacco but "big tobacco." The smell was very typical. Their delight, their joy, their leaping about, evidenced the quick pleasures of marijuana. Each pulled at the dregs in turn, and yelled "Bom Kali, Calcuttawali." I had never imagined that a marijuana container could be so alluring. The bright yellow kalki flowers which lent it their shape would also feel shamed. I realized that even these souls possessed the aesthetic sense that a container of intoxicants should be beautiful.

At first I was amused by the inebriated antics of my palki bearers, but gradually I grew irritated. As they smoked container after container, not one seemed interested in pressing ahead. When I asked when they would be done smoking, their leader answered – "Master, if they are not pulled up, they will not go. There is fear ahead, that's why they are looking for courage in marijuana."

I asked, "What fear?"

He replied, "Master, one must not put a name to that fear. You will see it a little later with your own eyes." On hearing this, I was so consumed by curiosity that I went myself to see if I could get the bearers going again. I saw that their eyes, so far yellow because of their diseased livers, had now, due to the intoxicant, turned as red as lime mixed with turmeric. I had to individually pull each and every one of the men to their feet. As a consequence I had to inhale a certain amount of the intoxicating smoke myself. This entered my nasal cavity and rose to my head. At once my body felt queasy, my extremities tingled, my eyes were strained and heavy. I quickly took shelter in the palki. It began to move again. This time I did not experience the suffering of riding in it, because I felt that my body was not mine but belonged to someone else.

A little while later – I cannot say how long it was – the bearers began to call out loudly in unison. I had already acquired evidence of the fact that their voices were more powerful than their bodies but that this power was of such magnitude, I realized for the first time. One word could be heard clearly through the hullaballoo – the name of Ram. Gradually, even their leader joined in with the incessant cry,

• PRAMATHA CHAUDHURI •

"Ram naam satya hai, Ram's name is the truth." I felt as if I were dead, and that ghosts were carrying me to their world in a palki. Whether the marijuana fumes had influenced such thoughts I cannot tell. I felt a great curiosity to learn where I was being taken. I looked outside and saw the sky aflame, like a village on fire. But of the attendant details of a conflagration – the cries and laments – I heard nothing. So desolate, so silent was the landscape, it seemed as if death's unshakeable stillness had cast a pall over the hustle and bustle of the world. The palki went a little further and I saw a desert ahead – not of sand but scorched earth. There was not a blade of grass upon it. No habitation graced this land, but there was proof aplenty that it had once before.

As far as the eye could see, I saw only bricks, more bricks, heaped in some places, scattered in the thousands in others – bricks so red it seemed as if fresh blood had congealed on them. Trees jostled out of this devastated habitation to reach for the sky; but not one had leaves, all were bald, dry, dead. These skeletal trees stood grouped together in some places, and in others leaned unsteadily, in ones and twos. And, all these bricks, the earth, and the sky seemed enveloped in fire, the colour of blood. It was not surprising that my bearers, being the sort they were, were frightened, since I too had begun to feel apprehensive. After a little while, from the depths of this silence a faint cry came to my ears. A cry so soft, so pleading, so timid, that it seemed as if aeons of accumulated human suffering resided within it. My heart overflowed with compassion at this cry, I felt a surge of empathy with all human sorrow. Just then a sudden storm arose, and a wild wind began to blow in from all sides. Urged on by the wind, the fire in the sky began to race crazily in all directions. Waves of fire billowed everywhere, and it seemed as if a hurricane had churned the blood-river in the sky. In that flaming inferno I saw the shadows of a

• SACRIFICE BY FIRE •

multitude of men and women, restless and writhing. On seeing this the winds began to clap their hands, and laugh out loud, "Ha ha ho ho!" Gradually this celestial noise merged into a roar of laughter – the sound of that cruel and pitiless laugh reverberating like waves in all directions. Then the laughter faded away and again I heard that soft, pitiful and timid cry. The strife between this hideous laugh and the soft cry aroused in my mind the history of this ruined city – whether those memories were of this life or of an earlier one I cannot say. From within me a voice confided, this was the history of the village.

This desert of bricks is all that remains of Rudrapur. The Rays of Rudrapur were once the most powerful landowners in the region. Rudranarayan, the founder of the Ray lineage, had worked for the Nawab and acquired the title of Ray as well as the ownership of three parganas. People say that the family possessed a self-signed seal of the Moghul Emperor and therefore his protection. But that they plundered and murdered, whether because of the seal or otherwise, there remains no doubt. Legend has it that landlords of such power and status had never before been seen in this region.

Their might and power was such that even the greatest of foes, as unlike as the goat and the tiger, were forced to exist together peacefully. Those who angered them, would risk having their life and property completely destroyed. They had laid countless homes to waste. There was no one within forty miles brazen enough to refuse their orders. Their harsh reign erased all traces of robbery, dacoity or even rioting in the land. A reason for this was that all the brutes in the area – the cudgel-wielders, spear-throwers and archers – had found employment as henchmen of the Rays. Just as they set no limits to the tortures they

---

A **pargana** is an administrative division in rural India.

inflicted upon their subjects, there was no end to the favours they bestowed. To hand out food and clothes to the poor, and medicines to the sick, was a part of their daily routine. There was no count of the many who were dependent on them. Their gifts of rent-free land to brahmans had turned many a priest into a tenant-farmer. And then they spent lavishly at religious festivals, at celebrations like Dol and at the annual festivities dedicated to Durga. During the former, the sky in Rudrapur would turn red with dye, during Durga puja the earth would run red with the blood of sacrificed animals. The guest house at Rudrapur was always equipped to feed at least a hundred guests. At rituals such as funerals and marriages no brahman ever walked away from the Rays' door empty-handed. The Rays would say, the wealth of brahmans is not to be hoarded – it is to be spent on meritorious works. Therefore, whenever they fell short in their charitable endeavours they did not hesitate to promptly loot some merchant's home to satisfy their ends. Simply stated, the good or evil that they did was subject to their whims and immediate desires, because there was no one to control them during the Muslim reign. As a consequence, the populace feared them as much as they revered them, since they themselves neither revered nor feared the populace. This unopposed rampage resulted in the Rays' gradual conviction of their own unquestioned superiority. They felt the pride of their caste, of wealth, of strength, as well as the pride of beauty. The men of the Ray family were all fair of skin, well-built and strong, while the beauty of their women was renowned throughout the land. For all of these reasons, for them to think of other humans as humans at all, had more or less become impossible.

    The Ray family had begun to fall apart before the English came to

---

Dol is the feast celebrated in Krishna's honour during spring.

• SACRIFICE BY FIRE •

India, and was almost gone by the time the East India Company came to rule. Those family members and shareholders who became destitute while the Rays grew in number, causing the property to be divided many ways, faded into oblivion. To earn wealth by one's own efforts, one's own labour, was in their opinion completely beneath their dignity. And then there were the quarrels within the family. The Rays were Saktas, beleivers in the goddess Kali – such fanatic Saktas that in Rudrapur old and young alike drank liquor. Even the women of the family raised no objection to this practice since they believed that imbibing liquor was a masculine thing to do. When, in the evening after worshipping the lion-mounted goddess Durga, the masters sat in the parlour and drank, the circle of red sandalwood on the foreheads of these enormous men, together with their hibiscus-red eyes, glared like the three anger-reddened eyes of the god Shiva. At such time there was probably no heinous act that they could not perform. They would instruct their henchmen to loot some shareholder's hoard of rice, or molest the women of some others. As a result, blood flowed. Because of all this family dispute, they reeled steadily to their own ruin. Because of the decennial ruling of the East India Company whatever remained of their wealth and property was transferred to other hands. It never occurred to them that Lakshmi, the goddess of wealth and well-being, would leave their household forever, if, on the final date, the last installment of revenue was not handed in at the Company's warehouse. To pay regular revenue was not something they had been used to doing during the reign of the Nawab. So now they were not quite able to meet the Company's demands for arrears. Consequently, most of their property was auctioned off to pay their overdue taxes. Simultaneously, the Ray lineage reached the point of extinction. The hundred households had been reduced, a hundred years ago, to only six landowners.

Gradually, even the property of these six households went into the hands of Dhananjay Sarkar. This was because Dhananjay not only knew the English laws well, but also abided by them. He knew not only how to use these laws to advantage, but also how to remain within their boundaries while garnering his wealth. He knew every trick at hand. As moktar, an attorney, in the district court of justice, he had earned immense amounts of money in barely a few years. Subsequently, as a money-lender, he doubled and trebled the interest, vastly increasing the principal. Rumour had it that in some ten years he had made ten lakhs of rupees. Even if it was not as much as this, there was no doubt that he was the owner of a few lakhs at least. After he had made his money, he wanted to acquire the status of landed gentry. To fulfil his desire he began to purchase, one by one, the properties of the Rays – because knowledge of every inch of this land lay at his fingertips. His ancestors had all worked for the Rays, and he himself, in his youth, had worked for the major shareholder of the remaining Ray family, Triloknarayan, as an accountant in his collectorate for some seven years. Even though he had acquired the lands as well as the households of all the Ray shareholders, he had not had the courage to go to Rudrapur as Ugranarayan, his master's son, was still alive. Ugranarayan, sacred thread in hand, had sworn upon the goddess that if Dhananjay ever stepped within the borders of Rudrapur during his lifetime, then he would not return alive. Dhananjay had no doubt that Ugranarayan would keep to every word of his promise. Because he knew that not even in the Ray family had one as indomitable and fearless as Ugranarayan been born before.

A few days after Ugranarayan's death, Dhananjay came to Rudrapur and took possession of the ancestral home of the Rays. By then not a single male member of the Ray family was alive, so, had he wished, he could have taken possession of all the houses of the shareholders. But he made no attempt to evict Ugranarayan's only daughter, the widowed Ratnamayi, from her father's house.

The reason for this was that the people of the Pathan neighbourhood next to Rudrapur had resolved to protect Ratnamayi's rights to the property. The whole village had, for generations together, armed men for this purpose; so Dhananjay knew that if he tried to evict Ratnamayi, bloodshed would be inevitable. He was extremely offended at this as he believed that, at that time, there was none to compare with his own gentle nature in all of Bengal. Another reason lay in his feelings of obligation and reverence for those who had supported him and his ancestors for generations. Because of this he spared Ugranarayan's share of the property but took over the rest of the original household of the Rays – though only in name.

Dhananjay's family consisted of his only daughter, Rangini Dasi, and Ratilal Dey, the son-in-law who lived with them. Once he had moved to his new home, Dhananjay underwent a noteworthy change – the more wealth he acquired, the greedier he became. In fact, he was consumed by a single emotion, greed. So he had been busy in blindly earning money any which way he could. He never stopped to think as to why, or for whom, he was doing this.

However, having moved to Rudrapur as a landlord, Dhananjay was struck by the sudden realization that he had been earning money for the sole purpose of acquiring wealth, not for anyone else or any other reason. He remembered that when, one by one each of his seven sons had died, he had not felt disturbed from his pursuit of wealth for even a day. This life-long avarice, had now, in his old age, grown into an obsessive attachment for his wealth. So obsessed was he with safeguarding his riches forever that he could not sleep at night. Rudrapur stood as manifest evidence that time can bring immense splendour to naught. Gradually, he came to the conclusion that while a man earns money through his own efforts, this wealth cannot be preserved without the assistance of the gods. Even though well-versed in English law, Dhananjay was essentially an uneducated man. His natural boorishness had never bowed to any form of education or systematic learning. His mind remained full of the Sudra mentality of the time, of blind beliefs and superstitions.

As a child Dhananjay had heard that if a brahman child was locked into a room full of treasures, that child, after it had died of starvation, would become a semi-divine being or Jakh and protect the wealth for ever. Gradually, he became convinced that it was his sole duty to procure a Jakh to protect his wealth. He was not used to having any compunctions about getting what he wanted, of transgressing any limits to achieve his ends. But in this case, he was faced with an enormous obstacle. On hearing that her father had resolved to thus sacrifice a brahman child, Rangini left off all sleep and food in protest. As a result, it became impossible for Dhananjay to fulfill his heart's desire. If there was *anything* that he loved other than his wealth, it was his daughter. Just as a tree might take root in a crevice in the masonry, so had love for his daughter found root in some crack in Dhananjay's hard heart. Even though Dhananjay was not instrumental in what was to transpire, the progress of events served to answer his final desires.

Ratnamayi had a three year old son – Kiritchandra. She lived alone, night and day, with this son in her house, she met no one, and no one was privileged enough to enter the inner chambers. The people of Rudrapur would have forgotten her existence had she not, every afternoon after her bath, gone to worship at the temple of the lion-mounted goddess. Two Pathan bodyguards would precede and follow her for her protection. Ratnamayi's age at the time was perhaps twenty or twenty one. Only one in a hundred thousand women was as regal as she.

Her figure was as beautifully proportioned as the lion-mounted goddess herself, and like her, her almond shaped eyes were level and steady. People said that they had never seen her eyes blink. What blazed in her eyes was a profound contempt for those who surrounded her.

Ratnamayi had inherited three centuries of her ancestors' accumulated arrogance. Needless to say, she was equally proud of her beauty, because her beauty was manifest evidence of her noble birth. To her mind, her beauty did not serve to attract people, but to censure them. When she would visit the temple, people on the road would stand aside, because her radiant complexion, and every limb and line of her body would silently reprimand them, "Begone! If you so much as step on my shadow I will have to bathe again." It goes without saying that she would look in no direction, but straight ahead, illumining the very path with her beauty as she went to the temple, and, in a similar manner, returned home. Rangini would look through her window and watch Ratnamayi everyday, and be consumed in her heart and soul by jealousy. Whatever else Rangini might have, she did not have beauty. Her lack of beauty grieved her greatly, more so because her husband, Ratilal, was an extremely handsome man.

Rangini loved her husband in the same manner that Dhananjay loved his wealth. Her love was no more or less than a profound hunger, and like the body's hunger, blind and pitiless. How much of a role her heart played in her love it is difficult to say because the hearts of creatures like Dhananjay and Rangini are a part of, not separate from, their bodies. And so, Rangini loved her husband the way that Dhananjay loved money, as if he were her property. The very thought that someone might lay hands on this property could drive all kindness, all compassion, from her. And there was no cruelty in the world that Rangini could not perform to keep that property to herself.

Quite without reason, a suspicion was born in her mind that Ratilal had been captivated by Ratnamayi's beauty. Slowly, that suspicion became a certainty as she suddenly discovered that Ratilal was secretly visiting Ugranarayan's house and spending as much time as he could there. The true reason for this was that Ratilal used to smoke marijuana with the brahman who had been given shelter at the house. Also, the childless Ratilal had developed such a great affection for Ratnamayi's son that he could not spend a day without seeing him.

Needless to say, he had never looked upon Ratnamayi herself because the Pathans guarded the doors to the inner chambers of the house. But Rangini grew more and more convinced that Ratnamayi, taken by Ratilal's good looks, had snatched him away from her. In revenge, and to satisfy her deep-seated jealousy, Rangini resolved to offer Ratnamayi's son as sacrifice. She informed her father one day that she no longer had any objections to his performing such a ritual. Not only this, but she would herself search for the boy. Of course, this task had to be accomplished in great secrecy.

So father and daughter consulted with each other and decided that the deed would take place in the chamber adjacent to Rangini's bedroom. Within a few days all the windows and doors of that room were sealed with bricks. Then, all of Dhananjay's hoard of gold and silver coins was placed there, in great secrecy, in rows of copper pots. When his entire wealth had been put in the room, Rangini implored Ratilal to bring Ratnamayi's son, saying that he was so beautiful that

Sacrifice By Fire

she had a great desire to hold and caress him. Thus she exhorted him, by whatever means, to bring the boy to her as soon as possible. Ratilal replied that it was impossible, for if Ratnamayi's guards came to know of this they would have his head. But Rangini was so persistent that, having no other course left open to him, Ratilal, one evening, coaxed Kiritchandra to come with him to see Rangini. As soon as Kiritchandra arrived, Rangini ran to him and placed him on her lap, kissed him and caressed him and spoke most sweetly to him. Then she draped a red silken wrap around his body, placed a garland of flowers around his neck, a spot of red sandalwood on his forehead and a gold bangle on each of his wrists.

Ratilal was elated to see Kiritchandra thus adorned. Suddenly, Rangini dragged the child by the hand, put him in the dark room, locked its doors from the outside and left. Ratilal, after attempting to push open one door after another, realized that Rangini had also imprisoned him, in their bedroom. He struck the door of the small chamber with his fists, kicked it with his feet and realized that his attempts to break down its door were futile. So heavy and so strong was the door, even an axe would not be able to cut through it. In his dark room Kiritchandra began first to sob, then to call out for Ratilal. After two or three hours the sounds of his cries subsided. Ratilal realized that the boy had cried himself to sleep.

Then, for three days and three nights Ratilal heard Kiritchandra sometimes beating his head upon the door, sometimes crying, and sometimes silent. In those three days the desperate Ratilal, not knowing what to do, charged at the door a thousand times each day. But it did not move even an inch. When he could hear the boy's cries, he would run up to the door and say, "My child, my child, don't cry like that, don't be afraid, I'm right here." On hearing

Ratilal's voice, the boy would cry out even more loudly, and repeatedly beat his head upon the door. Ratilal would then stop his own ears with his hands and run to the far corner of the room, scream out for Rangini, for Dhananjay, and curse out loud with whatever words came to his mind. He was so confounded by this devilish affair that it did not occur to him for a moment that there might be some other way to rescue Kiritchandra. His whole heart, rent by the boy's cries, lay captive in that dark little room. After three days, the child's cries grew soft, and feeble, and on the fifth day stopped completely. Ratilal realized that Kiritchandra's little life had come to an end. Then he pulled apart the iron bars on his window, jumped to the ground and ran to Ratnamayi's house. He saw that there were no guards that day at the doors of the inner chambers, that the Pathans were out searching for the boy in all directions. Ratilal took this opportunity to approach Ratnamayi and, in one breath, inform her of all the events that had occurred. For three years no one had seen Ratnamayi smile. On hearing of the cruel murder of her son her face and eyes lit up, as if she were laughing. This sight so appalled Ratilal that he ran from her and disappeared forever.

In the depths of that night – while everyone slept – Ratnamayi set fire to her house. The other shareholders' houses were closely clustered. So, within an hour that angry blaze, like the fury of the gods, spread to Dhananjay's house. Dhananjay and Rangini were attempting to flee, but arriving at the main gate, found themselves facing a hundred Pathans who surrounded Ratnamayi with their spears, shields and swords. On Ratnamayi's command, they fell upon the two, and, injuring them grievously, flung them into the raging flames. Ratnamayi immediately broke into a roar of loud laughter. Her companions realized that she had turned insane. The blood rushed to the heads of the Pathans, and they put to the sword Dhananjay's servants, officers, guards and messengers, whomever they found in front of them. A river of fire flowed over the ancestral household of the Rays', a river of blood beneath it. A storm arose, the earth began to shake. When everything had been reduced to ashes, Ratnamayi leaped into the flames herself.

Rudrapur had been destroyed. But Kiritchandra's cries and Ratnamayi's crazed laughter reverberate through the skies above it till this day.

---

[1] "Ahuti." From *Galpaguchha*, ed Sudhirchandra Sarkar, 4th ed, Oriental Press Pvt Ltd, Calcutta, 1965.

PANCHKARI DE

The Poet's Lover 5

I have always been powerfully drawn to the snow-capped, cloud-topped majesty of the Himalayas and so, one day, set out for the town of Darjeeling with my constant companion and bosom friend, Prabodhchandra.

On the way, we discussed our plans at length. Both of us were of the opinion that if we travelled by train, we would not be able to truly experience the Himalayas. Trains seem to fly past and it would be quite impossible, at such speeds, to absorb the breathtaking loveliness of the peaks. And so we decided that once we had reached the town of Siliguri, we would go on foot to Darjeeling.

We arrived at Siliguri in the morning. As long as the tiny beautiful train to Darjeeling remained in sight, we stood at the station watching it make its curious winding way along the mountain. Then, getting two coolies to carry our trunks on their heads, we slung our bags over our shoulders and set off for the market.

On the way to the market we met a couple of Bengalis. We had earlier decided to rent a room in the market, but they protested vigorously, insisting that we go to their house instead. The owner was a local businessman who dealt in timber.

We stayed that night in Siliguri. Everyone cautioned us, "Going by foot through the mountains will be most arduous, you'd better take a bullock cart instead." But we had made up our minds to walk. We had also decided not to walk along the main thoroughfare. It was far too crowded, with load-bearing bullock carts plying at all times. The rail tracks too, ran parallel to it for much of the way. It would be impossible to experience the sombre beauty of the Himalayas along it – and thus we were adamant not to go that way, even if our lives were at risk.

We decided, instead, to travel the meagre, narrow path taken by the hillfolk. However, mountain routes are treacherous and, moreover, we did not know the way. It was therefore essential to find ourselves a guide.

What can one not buy with money? With the assistance of our new friends we acquired a strong and trustworthy Bhutiya guide. He, in turn, arranged for three coolies whom he trusted. The following day, very early in the morning, the coolies loaded our boxes on their heads and we set off with a prayer in our hearts.

Walking ahead of us, two daggers at his waist, a hefty staff in his hand, was the Bhutiya Thambimena; following him, the two of us, and bringing up the rear, the three coolies. We crossed the bridge over the Mahananda river and then went beyond Matiyakhola, proceeding along the path to Naksabari.

Finding a shop selling provisions along the way, we stopped to cook and have a meal. There appeared to be no shortage of Marwari businessmen even in this remote place. At every few paces there were shops where one could get almost anything under the sun.

We rested awhile after our meal, then set forth again. It is not our intention here to elaborate upon the eternal loveliness of the mountains, or enthuse about that pinnacle of majesty, Sir Himalaya himself. So we shall speak no further on this matter.

It often happens in these parts that a sudden fog descends from nowhere to enshroud the land in darkness. At such a time one can see nothing at all – the mountain paths then have to be negotiated with difficulty and extreme caution.

The path we were on was a most treacherous one. On one side a deep ravine dropped thousands of feet below. Only one person could traverse the path at a time. Often we would have to crawl with difficulty on our hands and knees. We now began to climb cautiously upward in the mist-shrouded darkness.

It was nearly dusk by now, bitterly cold, and what was worse, it had begun to rain. If it hadn't been for the rain, the Himalayas might indeed have been the heavenly abode of the gods. If we could find a place to rest, we could spend the night there. We were weary to the bone. We could no longer determine where we were headed through the fog. Our guide declared that not far from here was another provisions store, and a village. But even after we had trudged on for an hour, no village appeared in sight.

The onset of evening is not as gradual in the Himalayas as it is where I come from. There is no such thing as twilight here. Suddenly, without warning, like a whimsical young girl, night swiftly drapes the mountains in its dark folds. We saw this for ourselves today, experienced the startling suddenness with which the land around became enveloped in a dense blackness that concealed everything.

Our guide proceeded, making strange noises in a shrill voice. We followed that sound as we awkwardly clambered along behind him. One missed step, and there we would be – plunging to a terrible death. We could now appreciate that our friends in Siliguri had indeed wished us well. But, what use is remorse on hindsight, if the dying patient himself refuses medicine?

Suddenly our guide stopped, and all of us abruptly came to a halt. We realized at once that he himself had lost his way in the dark – he had taken a path other than that leading to the village. And we had ended up in the remotest corner of that remote mountain. He had no idea what direction to take. Even if he did not admit to this in so many words, we sensed it in the tone of his voice.

It was then that our hearts sank. We realized that we had no choice but to spend the night in the thick jungle. That was, however, not as much of a problem – but only God's mercy could keep us from dashing to pieces in the depths of the ravine below.

Thambimena said, "If we turn back a little way along this path we will find a settlement."

We thought this a good idea, and anyway, had little choice in the matter, so we turned back. We had gone but a few steps, when I found myself at the edge of a slope. I don't quite remember what happened after that. I can't even recall how far I had tumbled. I soon realized that my good friend Prabodhchandra too, holding onto my long coat with both hands, was following my example and rolling down, right behind me. From the noise I realized that Gunwant Thambimena and the coolies had suffered the same fate – they were all tumbling down the slope.

Our fall was blocked suddenly by something in our path, that, on touch, seemed to be made of wood. I had a box of matches and a candle in my pocket. I took out the candle and lit it.

Candlelight did little to penetrate the darkness.

Holding the candle aloft I saw a wooden house. All three of us had been brought up short against its wooden fence. We picked ourselves up with some effort.

Anyway, we were relieved that we had escaped with our lives. Perhaps we could find shelter here. Whoever it was that lived in this house could hardly deny us refuge in this state. Holding the candle we found our way to the door, but found it closed.

I knocked – there was no answer. I knocked again, louder this time – again with no response. I then pushed at the door, which swung open with a creaking noise. The darkness inside the house was even thicker.

Holding up the light I stepped inside. Prabodh and Thambimena followed. But then an amazing thing happened. Thambimena let out a horrible yell and immediately ran out and disappeared into the night. Taken aback, Prabodh and I shouted after him but the only answer that floated back to us from the darkness was a terrified cry, which sounded to us like "The Devil's woman!"

Prabodh said, "Perhaps the locals believe that this house is haunted – the hillfolk are so superstitious! However, I thank God that we weren't killed when we fell down that steep ravine. I'm freezing in this cold – this shelter too, I'm sure, has been provided for us by Him. Let us gather some firewood now and get a fire going. Once they see the light, Gunwant Thambimena and his men will surely want to return."

We went outside and gathered some dry branches and twigs in the candlelight. After lighting a fire and warming our hands at it, we began to feel more like ourselves again. We always kept something to eat in our bags. Prabodh took the food out and began to tuck in with great alacrity. "Let us look around the room carefully first," I suggested. He said, "First, I would like to feel alive, and then all else! I'm dying of hunger. The high mountain paths and the dreadful cold have increased my appetite a thousandfold."

So we sat ourselves down in front of the fire and ate our fill.

After we were done, we took the candle and went off to search the house carefully. There were two rooms, not one, with various utensils lying around. It looked as if the last inhabitants of the house had, for whatever reason, left suddenly. Many of their possessions still lay around. Obviously, they had left in a hurry.

A box lay in a corner of the room. We noticed that the lid was open. Lifting it, we saw a number of letters, written in Bangla and with various dates.

It seemed, then, that some Bengali had come to live in this desolate and distant place. Who was he? And of all places, why had he come here? Consumed by curiosity we placed the candle on the box and began to read the letters one by one. As we came to the end of the final letter there arose from somewhere deep down a terrible, heart-rending cry that shattered the darkness. It sounded unceasingly through the night. We cannot say if this was a creation of our fevered imaginations, or a real human cry. We only know that we sat up all night, too terrified to even close our eyes.

Of those letters that we read, this was the first:

The First Letter

Dear Suresh,

I cannot tell you what peace I have found in these distant mountains, far from the dizzy whirl of Calcutta. I won't live in the city any more. I will not feel at ease there again, and so I have taken refuge in this remote place. How agitated my mind had been! No more, it is now calm. And where else but here, would I be able to contemplate in peace?

My house is situated in the midst of the mountains. Behind it, range follows range, rising to the sky, while in front, a little way off, lies a deep ravine at the bottom of which, some two thousand feet below, a river like a silver thread weaves its way.

There are only two rooms in this house. You can call them rooms, or anything you please. The wall is built of timber that has been bound together, so is the roof. There's no shortage of timber here – they grow everywhere – one can simply cut down what one needs.

I have no servants working for me – I've tried, but haven't managed to find any. Some four miles away there is a Bhutiya village, where a market is held once a week. On marketdays I set out in the morning, and come home by evening with my purchases.

I'm writing a long novel to pass the time. Perhaps this is the one that will make me world famous!

I've managed to find some help at last, but the man stubbornly refuses to stay here at night. Never mind, that isn't much of a problem. He finishes all the housework by day and goes back, so my wife doesn't have to work as hard as before.

At first she had been reluctant to stay in this lonely, remote place. I've explained to her that I will not be cured of my illness if I stayed in the city. And that finally made her more agreeable.

At night she sleeps in the other room. I sit in the front room and work late into the night on the magnum opus.

Yours,
Manmatha

The Second Letter

(The second letter spoke only of the novel, and was mostly full of praise for it.)

The Third Letter

Dear Suresh,

I've written two letters to you, this will make it three, but I've not been able to mail any of them. The post office is about twenty miles away and I've not yet been able to get a man to put these in the post.

There is a significant reason behind this. No one ever wants to venture this way, even if I pay them handsomely. I did not know why this was so until I asked an old man who explained the mystery to me. It is like this:

This cottage was built by a man named Shoho who was a poet of considerable repute among the Bhutiyas. He built his home in this desolate place so that he could stay in isolation, far from human habitation. He lived here with his lovely young wife.

Their days were happy until, unfortunately, a young Bhutiya woman who lived a short distance away, fell in love with the solitary poet. As I've mentioned already, this cottage has two rooms. When, at dead of night, the poet's young wife would be asleep in the other room, the other young woman would sit beside him and speak softly and sweetly of love.

One night the poet's wife stumbled upon the truth – but did not say a word.

The young woman had to cross a wooden bridge to reach the cottage. Some two thousand feet below, a waterfall gushed and roared, so fiercely that it had been named "Crazed Falls" by the Bhutiyas. Every night Shoho's lover would walk across the bridge over these falls.

One day, when Shoho wasn't home, his wife axed off the wooden stay at one end of the bridge. The bridge remained supported by so weak a link that the weight of a single person was sufficient to bring it crashing down.

That is what happened. That night, as always, Shoho was waiting for his lover when all of a sudden he heard a heart-rending scream. Immediately after, came the loud crashing sound of wood and stone – his lover had fallen to her death into the falls below.

THE POET'S LOVER

It did not take Shoho long to figure out who had done this deed. And because of this, Shoho and his wife too went to their deaths in that deep ravine.

Shoho had grabbed hold of his wife's neck to strangle her. But Bhutiya women are immensely strong and she managed to drag him to the edge of the ravine. He still did not take his hands off her neck. Her eyes rolled over, her tongue lolled, but she too did not let go of her husband. So they fell to their death two thousand feet below and were smashed to pieces.

"Since then," the old Bhutiya said, "Shoho's lover comes as a pret to this house. If she sees a light inside, she knocks on the door. No one has the power to keep her out. Many people have wanted to live here, but whoever does so, loses his life."

That is why no one has the courage to come here for fear of Shoho's ghost lover. I even have to get my own supplies from the market, and thus have not yet been able to mail these letters to you.

Yours,
Manmatha

The Fourth Letter

Dear Suresh,

If this had happened at home I would have laughed it off. I would probably have forgotten all about it within half an hour. But in the midst of this desolation it is not easy to scoff at ghosts.

Every night – into the small hours – I was working on that huge novel of mine. But after I heard the old Bhutiya's tale my writing has, in a manner of speaking, come to an end. You will laugh at me, but it's not right to hide the truth, and in fact, since that day when I first heard the story I began to put my pen down every so often, and to listen carefully for a knock at the door. It would seem that I was going out of my mind. However, in the meantime, something happened yesterday which has convinced me that I am indeed very disturbed, that I am indeed going mad.

I was strolling outside the cottage in the evening and chanced upon the broken bridge. I was peering over its edge to look at the rushing falls below, when I suddenly looked up to see a mountain lass resplendent in wild flowers, standing in the distance.

It had already begun to grow dark. I had never seen anyone, man or woman, so close to the cottage before. All other human habitation is more than four miles away. It is impossible to walk along these difficult mountain paths at night.

Who, then, was this young woman? Why was she here at this time? I cleared my throat to attract her attention but she did not move. I called out aloud, but she still did not respond. Thinking that she had not heard me, I waved my hand at her. At this, she slowly merged into the darkness. I turned towards home, rivers of ice flowing through my veins. I could not understand why I felt this way. Was it possible that she was not human, was this Shoho's lover?

Yours,
Manmatha

The Fifth Letter (Written eleven days after the previous letter)

Dear Suresh,

My premonitions have come true. She is here. Ever since I saw her in the mountains, I have known in my heart that she would surely come one day.

She came last night. We sat for a long time looking into each other's eyes.

You will surely say that I am insane – that my disease is not cured, that the fever is still upon me, that it holds my mind in its violent grasp – that it is my disturbed mind that imagines this wraith.

It is not only you, I've said this to myself many times over, yet, in spite of this, she has come. What is she – a woman of flesh and blood, or is she of the sky, a being of the air – a figment of my imagination? Whatever she may be, it is of little consequence. She is no illusion to me – not sky, not air, not false. She is real – very real!

She came last night. My wife was asleep in the other room, while I was working on my novel. I had waited every night for her – waited with anxious heart to hear her soft knocking at the door, counting each moment in eager anticipation. I can now well understand the condition of my mind.

I have heard her footsteps on the bridge, heard her clearly, knocking three times at the door – only three times.

On hearing it I felt as if a cold and icy stream had pierced my bones. My head throbbed with unspeakable pain. I clasped my arms tightly around my chest, but still that sound, that knocking at the door – three times, three times only. I listened carefully.

I stood up. Walking softly to the door of the other room I locked it, fastening the chain. And waited with baited breath. That sound again – knocking, three times, only thrice. I opened the door. A freezing wind rushed in and scattered my papers around, strewing some on the floor. The young woman stepped into the room, and I shut the door softly behind her.

She took her shawl off her head and draped it over her shoulder. She took out the coloured handkerchief which she had tucked in her bosom and then, facing me, seated herself near the fire. I saw her bare feet still wet with dew. I sat before her, gazing enchanted at her face.

She looked at me and smiled a sweet, soft smile – mysterious, yet somehow tinged with shrewdness, even treachery. At that smile I lost my heart! I no longer had any sense of right or wrong. I would give her everything – sacrifice for her all that I had!

She did not speak, did not even move. I felt no need to hear her speak. Those eyes full of desire, that wanton glance, what confidences of the heart did they not share with me. She looked at me, and I at her, our eyes met, what bliss, what delight – I do not have the power to describe it in words!

I do not remember how long I sat like that. Suddenly she raised a hand to her breast and listened carefully. At about the same time, I heard a very soft sound from the other room. At once she wrapped her shawl around her head and stood up, and then with swift steps opened the door and left, closing it behind her.

I opened the latch to the other room, laid my ear to the door and listened carefully – I heard nothing. Then I sat down. After that, I think, I fell asleep right there.

As soon as I woke up I remembered that the young woman had left her handkerchief behind. I had seen it where she had been sitting even after she had left. Wanting to conceal it, I looked for it as soon as I awoke. It was not there. My wife had swept the floor and cleaned the room, and had also put on some water to boil for tea. She looked at me once or twice – I had never seen her look at me like that before. But she did not say a word, nor did she mention the handkerchief.

I was almost convinced that the events of the night before had been a dream. But when I went out in the afternoon I saw my wife examining the handkerchief with great care. She was looking the other way and did not see me. But I could see how minutely she was looking at it.

I tried telling myself over and over that it was my wife's handkerchief. That the events of the night were only a figment of my imagination. And if it was not so, the person who had visited me last night was no ghost but an actual woman.

But one human can know another, and feel that presence as human. And my heart had sensed that the person who had sat in front of me the night before was not of flesh and blood.

Perhaps she was a real woman. But there is no human settlement within four miles of this place. It is dangerous enough to walk these mountainous paths by day – and quite impossible by night. What woman would risk walking here at the dead of night? That too in such dense darkness, such bitter cold ... Moreover, what woman would set my blood freezing and chill me to the bone by her mere presence?

Whatever it is, whoever it is, if she comes again I will speak to her just once. I will put out my hand and touch her. I will find out then if she is of flesh and blood, or simply of the air – a creature of my imagination, a vacuum, or a shadow.

Yours,
Manmatha

The Sixth Letter

Dear Suresh,

I have lost hope that you will ever receive these letters. I will not send you these letters from here. You will think of them as the ravings of a madman, the insane babbling of a crazed mind, nothing more. If I ever return home I might someday show these letters to you, but it won't be in the near future. When I return and am able to laugh and joke about all this, only then will I show you these letters. I now write these to you as I'm in great mental anguish. If I do not write like this,

I would probably have to scream out loud to ease my suffering.

She comes in every night, sits by the fireside, looks into my eyes – and smiles that enchanting soft, sweet smile. My head begins to churn, I am lost in her – I exist no longer!

My work on the novel has ground completely to a halt – I don't even try to write any more. I wait in agony for the sound of her footsteps on the bridge, on the grass, her soft knock at the door.

And when she comes, every time it is the same – I cannot speak a word – I am not myself – I can think of nothing. She does not speak either, she just looks at me as she always does, smiles as she always smiles.

Each day I think, when she comes this time, I shall certainly speak to her, I shall certainly touch her. But the moment she arrives I forget everything, I lose myself completely.

Last night, as I was looking at her face, my heart overwhelmed by her amazing beauty, her lips opened slightly, and she stood up startled. I looked at the window of the other room and it seemed as if someone had suddenly withdrawn her face from the window. In a moment she had pulled her shawl over her head and swiftly left the house.

I took the candle and went to the next room. I found my wife asleep.

Yours,
Manmatha

The Seventh Letter

Dear Suresh,

I don't fear the night, it is the day that I'm afraid of. I now hate with all my heart the woman I have always called my wife. It is all-consuming, boundless. All her devotion and care is now anathema

The Poet's Lover

to me. I shudder in horror when I look at her eyes – Lord alone knows why.

I now know that she has seen everything, has come to know all.

Yet she still loves me, with care, with affection – with devotion, even. Even then I feel that this is all an illusion, my fancy, a deception – that we are, in fact, both plotting our revenge against each other.

The Eighth Letter

Dear Suresh,

I set out this morning for the market. My wife remained standing at the door as I walked further and further away. I turned back once and saw her standing there, as tiny as a doll. Finally, as I went around the mountain, I could see her no longer.

I then ran back towards the house as fast as I could, along a different path, stumbling and picking myself up as I ran. Such haste is not easy along these paths, and I fell down often before I reached the house. Then I hid behind a large rock and watched the house.

A little later I saw my wife approach the wooden bridge with an axe. From where I was I could not see clearly what she was doing. She stood up after a while. I saw her smile even at that distance – and it seemed to me that her smile blazed with the fire of revenge.

I headed for the market again after she had returned to the house. When I returned in the evening she greeted me with her usual affection.

I was especially careful to conceal the fact that I had seen her dreadful act. Let her devilish deed remain that way. She must have thought that a woman walked across the bridge every night to speak words of love to me, and so had hacked away the supports of the bridge. She hoped that today, when my lover came to me, she would fall to her death into the ravine.

I did not utter a word. Today I will find out for sure who it is that comes to me every night. If she is a spirit then the fall of the bridge will not hurt her. But if she really is human, then ...

I banished this last thought from my mind. To think of it made me shudder in horror.

If she is human then why does she look at me in silence? And why can I not ask her a thing? Why do I lose myself in her presence? Surely she isn't human. My wife will not be able to harm her in any way. That wretch will burn even more at her fruitless revenge. It will serve her right.

But if she belongs to the world of the dead, how is it that I can hear her footsteps? See clearly the drops of dew on her feet? How do I hear the sound of her knocking on the door? These are not the signs of a spirit.

It is night and my wife is asleep in the next room. I wait eagerly in the front room, listening for the sound of my lover's footsteps.

If she is an inhabitant of the nether world, then she will, as before, come to me, and if she is human, then I will surely hear her scream as she falls into the ravine. Is a spell from some unknown world engulfing me in its illusion?

Suddenly ... oh what ghastly mockery is this!

I have heard – I have just heard that terror-filled scream, that heart-wrenching cry, shattering the firmament.

Cleaving sky and earth, rending the night asunder, that dreadful cry rose from near the bridge, from that fathomless ravine and echoed off the mountain peaks. That cry is still resounding in my ears, surging with the blood through my veins!

I rushed out to the bridge. I lay on the ground and stretched out my arm – the bridge was gone.

I looked down, in that dense darkness – into the black cavernous depths. I could see nothing.

The wind was strong. I screamed out to her ... in that raging wind my cry shook the horizon, reverberating like the shrill laughter of some demoniac being.

I now understand. The madness that has been slowly but surely increasing its powerful grip on me – there is no other way – it is useless to fight ... useless ... useless ...

I keep telling myself that this is some fancy of my diseased mind – this scream is in my imagination. No ... no ... no ... there is that sound again! There is that scream! That heartbreaking cry!

I feel as if someone is pounding my head with a heavy iron hammer. I realized then that she would come to me no more. This was the end!

Yours,
Manmatha

The Last Letter

Dear Suresh,

I will leave all these letters in a large envelope with your address on it. If anyone ever comes here and finds them, perhaps he will send them to you.

I no longer read or write. We – my wife and I – I have to call her my wife to explain to you who I am referring to – we sit looking at each other, not speaking a word. What a strange turn of events.

When we do speak, it is as if we are strangers. Even the few words that we utter, are really a smokesrcreen for what we conceal in our hearts. Neither of us is the person we used to be. I see always on her face the mockery behind her smile. She tries to hide it, but I can see through her. Her attempts are useless!

Every night as I sit alone, I imagine that she is knocking at the door as before. I run quickly to open the door, but no, there is no one, only the darkness – and a chilly wind that blows in from that black night and rushes into the room – nothing else at all.

This desolate place has made me into a demon. Love and hate both seem to fill my heart, to dart like lightning through my veins, to light a hundred funeral pyres inside my head. My studies, my education, my talents – all of this seems to have been borne away from my heart by the mountain wind. I have become a savage animal.

When will I – this woman, who used to be my wife – when will my skeletal emaciated-with-disease fingers close about her petal-soft throat. Her fine eyes will slowly close shut ... her mouth fall open ... her scarlet tongue loll out ... when will I tighten my hold on her neck, slowly, slowly, press down ever more deliberately! Not much longer ... not for long ... not much longer! Then, clutching her neck, I will push her away from the cottage ... drag her across the hard stones ... and bring her to the edge of the ravine. She smiled mockingly at me! It's now my turn to laugh. Ha! Ha! Ha ...

I will force her along slowly, even with affection – when she hangs over the precipice by a single toe, then I will lean towards her and kiss her on her bloodless lips. Then, down, down, down, through the fog, tearing through the shrubs and creepers, astonishing the animals and birds, down ... down ... deep down ... we will go together ... together ... until I meet with *her* again.

(This letter remained incomplete.)

This was the last letter – after reading these diabolic letters Prabodh and I looked at each other. What I saw on his face was probably what he saw in mine. His face had quite lost its colour.

• THE POET'S LOVER •

Neither of us found the courage to speak. Both our hearts were beating fiercely.

We had not known that such terrifying events could ever be possible in life. We now realized that our guide Thambimena had had reason enough to flee in fear.

We had never believed till now in ghosts and spirits. Whether there were such beings or not, the letter-writer Manmatha had, in this desolate place become fearsomely crazed with his obsessive thoughts of such beings. In his madness the unfortunate wretch had murdered his wife, and killed himself. These letters were proof to this.

We escaped from the wooden house as soon as it was light. Dear God! Who would have stayed there for a minute longer! When we reached the village we found our coolies and Thambimena. They were astounded to see us alive even after spending a night in that cottage and stared at us in amazement.

When we arrived in Darjeeling we handed over all the letters to the Commissioner. We have heard that, on his orders, that sinister cottage has been razed to the ground.

"Sarbanashini." From *Nirbachita Bhuter Galpo*, ed Ranjit Chattopadhyay, Ananda Publishers Pvt Ltd, Calcutta, 1992.

BIBHUTIBHUSHAN BANDOPADHYAY

In the Forest of Bomaiburu

Various sections of the forest were under survey. Our surveyor Ramchandra Singh had therefore been staying for a few days in the forest of Bomaiburu, some six miles from the head office. One morning, we received the news that two or three days ago, Ramchandra Singh had suddenly gone insane.

On hearing this I made for the forest at once, along with some men. The forest of Bomaiburu was not too dense – a few tall trees with thin creepers hanging from their branches, like ropes tied to the high mast of a ship, grew far apart from each other on an empty, undulating landscape. There was no human habitation in the Bomaiburu forest.

Far from the copse of trees, in an empty field, stood two tiny kash-thatched huts. The one in which our amin, the survey clerk Ramchandra babu, stayed was slightly bigger while the smaller one was for his peon, Asrafi Tindel. Ramchandra lay on his wooden bunk with his eyes shut. He scrambled up on seeing us. I asked, "What's up, Ramchandra? How are you?"

Ramchandra joined his hands in greeting but remained silent.

However, Asrafi Tindel answered the question. He said, "Babu, it's an amazing story. You won't believe me when you hear it. I would have gone down to the office myself to tell you but how could I have left Amin babu by himself? This is how it all happened.

"For some days Amin babu had been complaining of a dog that came and pestered him at night. Now, I sleep in the little hut, and

Amin babu sleeps here. For the past few days he had been saying, Lord knows where a white dog turns up from at night. I lie down on my bunk, and along comes the dog and whines beneath it, and tries to rub himself against me. I listened, but didn't bother much. Then, about four days ago, late at night, he called out, Asrafi, come out quick, the dog's here. I'm holding it fast by its tail. Get a stick along.

"I woke, and running up with a stick and light, I saw – you will not believe this, Master, but I would not have the courage to lie in your presence – a young woman coming out of the room and walking towards the forest. I was bewildered. Then, on entering the room I saw Amin babu groping about on his bed for matches. He asked, Did you see the dog?

"I said, What dog Babu? It was a girl that went out.

"He said, You monkey, are you trying to be impertinent with me? What woman would come to this forest in the middle of the night? I had the dog by its tail, and even felt its long ears brush against me. It was whining under the bunk. Have you taken to drink? I shall report you to the authorities.

"The following day I stayed alert late into the night. Just as I had nodded off, Amin babu called out. I had barely managed to reach the threshold of my room when I saw a girl climbing over the fence to the north of his room and going towards the forest. I immediately went into the jungle myself, Babu. In that short span of time, where could she hide and how far could she go? Since we survey the forest, we know every inch of it. How I searched, Master, but could find no trace of the woman. Then, a sudden suspicion gripped my mind. I turned the light towards the ground, but saw no footprints except those made by my own nagras.

"I said nothing of this to Amin babu that day. Two beings alone in

• In The Forest Of Bomaiburu •

this terrible forest, Babu. Fear raised goose bumps on my skin. And I had heard somewhat of Bomaiburu's ill-fame from my grandfather. Do you see that far-off banyan tree on Bomaiburu hill? Well, one moonlit night my grandfather was returning on horseback with his earnings from Purnea, when, under that very banyan, he saw a group of young and beautiful girls holding hands and dancing under the moon. In these parts they call them damabanu – evil fairies who live in lonely forests. If they happen to chance upon someone who has lost his way, they may even kill him.

"Hujoor, the following night, I went to Amin babu's tent myself and stayed awake the entire night working on the survey lists. Perhaps I had dozed off towards the end when I suddenly heard a noise and looked up. I saw Amin sahab sleeping on his bed, and something creeping in under it. I peered under the bed and was startled. In the half-light half-shadow it seemed as if a girl sat crouched under the bed, smiling up at me. I saw this clearly, Hujoor, I swear to you. I even saw the thick black hair upon her head distinctly. My lantern stood some five or six feet away, where I had been working on the lists. Wishing to see more clearly what I thought I saw, I went to fetch the lantern. At once something ran out from under the bed and tried to escape. The light from the lantern fell at a slant near the doorway. In that light I saw a large dog, white from tip to toe Hujoor, with not a speck of black on it.

"Amin sahab woke up and said, What? What? I said, Nothing, a fox or a dog had come into the room. Amin Sahab said, A dog? What kind of dog? I said, A white dog. In a tone of despair Amin sahab said, Are you certain you saw a white dog? Not black? And I said, No, Hujoor, it was white.

"It was not as if I wasn't rather astonished. How did it matter to Amin babu if the dog was black instead of white? He went back to sleep – but I felt fearful and uneasy and could not sleep a wink. I woke up very early, and, on a sudden hunch, searched carefully under the bed and found a lock of black hair. Here it is, Hujoor. It's the hair of a woman. Where did it come from? Soft jet-black hair. A dog – especially a white dog, cannot have such long, soft, black hair. This was last Sunday, about three days ago. Since then Amin sahab seems to have become deranged. I am scared, Master ... I wonder if it is my turn now."

This was quite a fantastic story. I examined the lock of hair myself, but could deduce nothing. That it was the hair of a woman, I had no doubt. Asrafi Tindel was young, but everyone vouched for the fact that he did not drink or take drugs.

The uninhabited terrain and forest shrubs held only one tent, Amin babu's. The nearest habitation was Labtulia village, some six miles away. Where could a woman have come from, that late in the night – especially when, in such a desolate place, people do not venture out after dusk for fear of tigers and wild boar?

If I took Asrafi Tindel's story to be true, then the affair was extremely mysterious. Or else, it seems that this godforsaken land, deserted forest and barren stretch of country is untouched not only by the twentieth century, perhaps even by the nineteenth. The land was still enshrouded in the mysterious darkness of hoary age – and all seemed possible.

Having packed up the tents in the forest I brought Ramchandra Amin and Asrafi Tindel to the town office. Ramchandra's condition deteriorated by the day and he became increasingly demented. He would rage throughout the night, alternately screaming, blabbering, and singing. I brought in a doctor to see him, but to no avail. Finally, an elder brother of his came and took him away.

There is a conclusion to this tale, though it took place some seven

• IN THE FOREST OF BOMAIBURU •

to eight months after this incident. Even so, let me speak of it here.

About six months after these incidents, in the month of Chaitra, two men came to meet me in my office. One of them was old, not less than sixty or sixty five. The other, his son, was about twenty or twenty two. Their home was in Balia district and they had come to lease pasture land from us, that is, they were to pay rent for permission to put their cows and buffaloes to graze in our forest.

All of the other pasture lands had already been leased out, only the Bomaiburu forest remained. I arranged for them to take it on lease. The old man and his son even went to see the place for themselves. They were delighted, saying the grass was tall and plentiful and the forest a good one. Had the Hujoor not been so kind they would never have found such a fine forest.

I did not, at the time, remember the incident concerning Ramchandra Amin and Asrafi Tindel. Even if I had, I probably would not have said anything to the old man, because had he taken fright and left, the landlord would have suffered a loss. The locals would have nothing to do with the forest, especially after the Ramchandra Amin episode.

One day, a month or so later, at the onset of Baishakh, the old man presented himself at the office, looking furious, while his son stood cowering behind him.

I asked him what the matter was.

Trembling with rage, the old man said, "I have brought this ape to you to judge! Take the shoes off your feet and beat him, let him learn a thing or two!"

Baishakh is the first month of the Bengali calendar, from the middle of April to the middle of May.

"Why, what is it?"

"I'm ashamed to speak to Hujoor about this. This ape, ever since he's come here, has been getting out of control. For the past seven or eight days I've been observing – I'm ashamed to admit this, Hujoor – a woman leaving his room. Both of us sleep in this tiny thatched hut, some eight feet in length and it is not easy to fool me. When I observed this for a couple of days, I asked him what he thought he was up to. He seemed bewildered and denied all knowledge of the woman. When I saw this happen on two more occasions, I gave him a good hiding. Will my son go to the dogs right before my eyes? But when I saw things even after that day, just this night before last, Hujoor – I brought him to you. Now you discipline him."

Suddenly I remembered the Ramchandra Amin affair. I asked, "At what time of the night did you see this?"

"As the night came to an end, Hujoor. When one or two hours of the night were left."

"Are you sure you saw a woman?"

"Hujoor, my eyes haven't grown that feeble yet. I'm certain it was a woman, quite young, sometimes dressed in a washed, white saree, at times red and at times black. One day, as soon as she left, I followed her. I could not make out where she ran off into that kash forest. When I returned, I saw my son pretending to be sound asleep. He scrambled up when I called him, as if he had just woken from deep sleep. I knew then that he could not be set right without getting him to the office, so I have brought him here to you ..."

I took the boy aside and asked him, "What is all this I hear about you?"

The boy threw himself at my feet and pleaded, "Please believe what I say, Hujoor. I know nothing of all this. All day I tend the buffalo herds in the forest – at night I sleep like the dead, and wake up only in the morning. Even if the hut caught fire I would not know it."

I asked, "You have never seen anything enter the room?"

"No, Hujoor. I lose all sense when I sleep."

Nothing further was said about this. The old man was very pleased, thinking I had taken the boy aside and given him a severe talking to. About fifteen days later the boy came to me. He said, "Hujoor, I have to speak to you. The day I came to you with my father, you had asked me if I had seen anything come into the room."

"Well, what about it?"

"Hujoor, I sleep very lightly these days – perhaps because my father suspects me of all sorts of misdoings, perhaps because of fear, or something. Well, for the last few days I've been seeing a white dog that seems to appear out of nowhere – it comes late at night. Some nights I wake up and find it near the bed. As soon as I wake up it runs off – it seems to sense that I'm awake. This has been going on for a few days. But last night something happened, Hujoor. My father knows nothing of this. I have come here without his knowledge to talk to you. Late last night I woke up and saw the dog – I hadn't seen it come into the room – it was now trying to slink out. There is a gap in the kash hedge the size of a window. As the dog went out of the room, in the blink of an eye, I saw a woman pass by my window at the back of the house. I ran outside at once – I could see nothing. I did not say anything to my father, he is old, and was sleeping. I cannot figure out what is happening Hujoor."

I reassured him, "Oh, it's nothing, just a delusion." I also said that if they were afraid to sleep out there they could come and sleep in the office. The boy seemed somewhat embarrassed at his own lack of courage, and left. But my discomfort remained, and I decided that if

I heard anything further from them I would send over a couple of guards from the office for the night.

But I had not realized then how critical the matter was. The mishap struck most suddenly and unexpectedly.

Three days later.

I had just got out of bed that morning when I received the news that the old cowherd's son had died in the Bomaiburu forest. We mounted our horses and set off at once. On arriving, we saw the boy's dead body still lying in the kash and tamarisk forest behind their hut. The boy's face was frozen in an expression of immense fear and terror – as if some ghastly apparition had terrified him to death. I came to know from the old man that on not finding his son in bed late at night, he had at once picked up a lantern and begun to search for him. But not until dawn had he discovered his son's body. Probably the boy had suddenly got out of bed to follow something into the forest because, next to his body, lay a thick stick and a lantern. What he had followed at that time of night into the forest it is difficult to say, for, on that soft sandy soil there were no footprints – human or animal – other than his own. Nor did the body bear any signs of injury or assault.

This mystery of the Bomaiburu forest was never solved. The police came but returned when they found nothing. The event struck such terror in the hearts of the local people that they would avoid the area long before the sun set. For some days it even happened that, lying alone in my room in the office, looking out at the pale, shadowless, desolate moonlit night, I would tremble with an unknown dread. I would want to rush back to Calcutta, for I had actually begun to believe that these places were evil, and that indeed, like the Demon Queen of fairy tales, the charmed and silvery night could put you under her spell and kill you.

• In The Forest Of Bomaiburu •

As if such places were not meant for humans to inhabit, but were the exclusive domain of disembodied and sinister beings from the world beyond who had lived there through the ages. And who, when enraged by the rude and sudden tresspassing of man into their secret space, sought every opportunity to wreak revenge.

---

[1] "Bomaiburur Jangale." From *Nirbachita Bhuter Galpo*, ed Ranjit Chattopadhyay, Ananda Publishers Pvt Ltd, Calcutta, 1992.

TARASHANKAR BANDOPADHYAY

The Witch

Though the person who first coined its name has long been lost to the oblivion of history, the name survives in all its resplendence. Standing at one end of the vast, seemingly endless expanse of Chatiphata, the land without shade, without water, one sees, at the other, some signs of habitation: a village, with trees that appear as if moulded from plaster. One's mind grows strangely desolate. The prospect of dying of thirst whilst traversing the length of Chatiphata is not unlikely, especially in summer. At such a time Chatiphata appears voracious enough to measure up to its name, to equal the death-dealing onslaught of an epidemic. A grey blanket of dust, like dense smoke, rises from the earth to the sky. The dark outlines of the distant village become all but invisible. Chatiphata becomes then, a thing of fear, a place strange and unknown. Over it floats a pall of grey smoke, while the field itself, leafless and barren, resembles the scorched remnants of a burnt-out pyre. Heaps of pale soft dust lie gathered almost a foot deep. Trees there are few – some brown thorn shrubs, perhaps, strewn here and there. There are no large trees – these do not grow here. There is no water. The few ponds lie like barren wombs, thinly scattered over Chatiphata.

Around the field lie small villages, the homes of illiterate people. These homes do not know how to keep a secret. It is said, in some ancient time a great serpent came to live in Chatiphata. And that,

---

[1] **Chatiphata** literally means something which rends one's chest with pain, or suffering.

because of its venom, the land which had once been capable of yielding a lush vegetation, became as dry as ash. It is said that, at the time, birds flying above Chatiphata would suddenly lose the strength in their wings and like dry leaves swirling in the wind, fall to the ground.

The serpent is long gone, but the power of its venom remains. Chatiphata continues to lie under a spell. Another misfortune now afflicts the land. Someone cast an unfeeling, merciless eye upon it. For some forty years now, to the east, upon the turgid and muddy swamp where the Sahas of Ramnagar have their mango grove, lives a witch – a powerfully malevolent old witch. The village folks shun her. But, having seen her every now and then (albeit from a safe distance) for forty years, they can describe her every feature, especially how her gaze is steady and unblinking, and how it has been turned upon this land for forty years.

In the shadow of the mango grove, upon the swamp itself, stands a mud hut facing Chatiphata. In front of its door is a straw-roofed veranda. An old woman sits upon it and gazes, unblinking, at the land. There are two things that she considers as work – she cleans her home and plasters it with cowdung. Then she leaves for the village to beg for alms. This part of her work is accomplished quickly. Just two or three houses and she has enough for her needs, for the people fear to give her too little. As soon as she has about a seer of rice, she returns home. On the way back she sells half the rice and buys a little salt, a little cooking oil and some kerosene. Then she goes out once more to forage for clumps of dried cowdung and twigs. After this, she sits in silence at her door. She has been staring at the land for forty years now.

The old woman has not always lived here – no one knows where she comes from. However, it is known for a fact that having completely destroyed three or four other settlements, travelling along the sky

· THE WITCH ·

upon a tree, she was attracted by the desolation of Chatiphata. Here she descended, and made it her home.

Women such as she relish their solitude, they do not desire the company of mortals. For as soon as she looks upon humans, her heart fills with murderous desire. The destructive and pernicious force in her raises its hood like a cobra, that dancing, flicks its tongue.

Seeing her own reflection in an ancient mirror, she cowers at the sight of her eyes – hungry eyes in which two tawny stars burn, a gaze as sharp as a gleaming knife. Decrepit and wrinkled of face, hair as white as snow, a toothless mouth. Her lips tremble at the sight of herself in the mirror. She sets it aside. The wooden frame around the mirror has grown dark with age – yet what a beautiful red it had been once, of such polish! And the glass – as bright as a pond in sunlight. A face could once see itself so clearly in that mirror. A small forehead, surrounded by thick hair, not black, but of a reddish tint; a sharp nose curving gently from the forehead; the eyes small – their pupils yellow – people feared to look at those eyes. But she loved her eyes. She thought she could gaze into the depths of the sky even if she did not completely open her small eyes. Suddenly she shivers – these eyes split as if with a razor, eyes like knives, cats' eyes – those whom these eyes look upon and desire can find no place to hide. What befalls them, how it happens, she does not know; all she knows is that it does.

She remembers the first time.

She was standing on the broken embankment of the Durgasayor pond, in front of Buroshibtala. Her inverted reflection lengthened and rippled with the waves in the pond. When the water grew still, it reflected a ten or eleven year old girl laughing back at her. All of a sudden Haru Chowdhury of the brahman household caught her by her hair and flung her to the ground on the stone steps leading down to the pond. She could still hear the harsh voice in her ears – "Wretched witch, why are you casting an evil eye at my son? Who do you think you are? I'll kill you!"

The fearsome image of Haru still floated before her eyes.

Distraught with fear, she'd screamed out – "Master, spare me! Spare me! I beg your mercy!"

"If you were greedy for some puffed rice with mango, why didn't you say so, you wretch?"

True, she had wanted it, she had wanted it so much her mouth had filled with water!

"Wretch! My son is thrashing around with a stomachache!"

She often wonders, even today, how such a thing came about. But she no longer has any doubts that Haru spoke the truth. She remembers clearly, how she had gone to Master Haru's house and wept copiously, how she had prayed silently for his son, "God, make him well, make him well." How many times she had declared in her mind, "I'm taking my evil eye back, here it is." Amazingly, in a short while, after vomiting a couple of times, the boy's condition had improved and he had fallen asleep.

The Master had asked that she be given some puffed rice and a mango.

His wife had brandished a broom at her and said, "I'll smear your face with ashes. An orphan girl, that's why I pity her. Whenever she comes she gets something. And she casts her evil eye upon my son! Look at her standing there, listening! Those eyes, I always suspected her, I never let my children eat with her. And today, I give Khoka his

---

Smearing someone's **face with ashes** implies humiliation or to cause someone or something to be ineffective.

· THE WITCH ·

food and go to the pond, and she comes and stands before him! Look at her eyes!"

She had fled from there in shame and fear. That night, she was not allowed to sleep at anyone's door in the village. She slept on its outskirts in Buroshibtala. All night she had wept, and prayed, "O God, cure me, or make me blind!"

A deep sigh shakes the motionless body of the old woman. Her lips start to tremble.

There is no thwarting the sins of a past life – neither is it the fault of the gods, nor can they help it! She remembers she had decided never to enter the home of a householder again. She began begging at the outer gates, hardly able to speak, mumbling, "Ma, give me some alms! Praise God!"

"Who's that? Oh, is it you? Don't you dare come inside. Don't you dare!"

"No, Ma, I'm not coming in."

But, just then, something would writhe and wriggle in her mind – as it still did. Oh, the delightful smell of frying fish! It must be a large, ripe fish!

"Here! Here! Shameless wretch! Look at her peeking in! Like a snake."

For shame. To tell the truth, she had been peeking – she had cast a look on everything laid out in the kitchen with a single sweep of her razor-slit eyes. Water rose in her mouth like a spring.

The wan old woman, standing like a clay image moulded aeons ago, feels a tremor pass through her body. Her aging joints move restlessly as she shudders. She shifts her position – the nails at the end of the long, thin fingers of her left hand leave marks on the mud floor. She has spent a lifetime trying to understand how this could have happened, how this came about. But what was she to do? Could anyone tell her what she should do, what she could do? Like a beast that has been beaten and left for dead rises suddenly to call out, the old woman lets out a shrill cry, shakes her mane of hair and stands up erect. Clamping her toothless gums together, she stares at Chatiphata with her razor-sharp hawk's eyes, and begins to pant.

Chatiphata appears covered in a haze of smoke. It is the month of Chaitra, the day is no longer young. Something that sparkles and twinkles runs through the haze. If she lets out a sudden scream, the heaps of dust will become airborne.

What is that white, dense thing that moves in the haze? Is it human? Yes, it is. Her mind stirs uneasily. Will she blow the dust away, and the human with it? Giggling crazily, like a madwoman, she feels a cruel curiosity beginning to arise in her.

With all her strength, she clenches her fists and tries to force her mind to obey, to bring it to order – no, no, no. That man will perish of heat and breathlessness, from lack of breath, on Chatiphata.

No, she will not even look in that direction. Instead, she will sweep her porch of fallen leaves and twigs, a better idea. She gets down on her haunches and sweeps the veranda, dragging her broken old body.

The gathered leaves suddenly rise up like a serpent and, twisting and turning, begin to fly about. Dust mingles with the leaves, and seems to embrace the old woman, getting into her eyes and mouth, harassing her, fretting about her, the swiftly turning leaves seeming to strike her. Like an old, hairless, wounded female cat, she grimaces angrily, flings the broom aside, and cries, "Go away! Go away!"

Again and again she strikes at the vortex of air, which eddies away over the field. The wind gathers the dust over the field into a swirling pillar. Not just one but countless whirlpools of dust, rising and falling – as if the field is mocking her – one becoming thousands. A strange excitement makes her restless. Suddenly, she picks up her bent body, and, with the broom still in her outstretched hand, begins to turn round and round as fast as she can. In a short while she is dizzy, and sits down. It seems as if the earth were flinging her off from some steep height to some depthless pit. She does not even have the strength to raise herself. She crawls like a baby towards the door. A desperate thirst assails her.

"Is someone at home?"

The old woman is lying at her door like a fallen branch, water-rotted and soft. At the sound of the voice she wearily raises her head and asks, "Who is it?"

A young woman, covered in grey dust, face pinched and pale with thirst, stands facing her. Beneath her saree she clutches something to her breast. She must have lost her way in Chatiphata. The girl looks down at where the voice is coming from and sees the old woman. She trembles in fear. Retreating hesitatingly, she pleads, "Just a little water."

Pushing down on the ground with one hand, the old woman manages to raise herself. Looking at the girl's pinched face, she exclaims, "Oh, you poor thing! Come, come here. Sit down."

Fearfully, and with great caution, the girl sits near the door, and pleads again, "Please, I need water!" The old woman's heart softens in compassion, she hastens inside and, filling a large pot with water, searches a jar for a piece of jaggery. She asks, "Whatever made you cross this monstrous field in such heat, my dear?"

Sitting outside, still panting from the heat, the girl says in a trembling, dry voice, "My mother is very ill. I left home while it was still night. However, I lost my way at the edge of the field. My route was to skirt Chatiphata, but somehow I have ended up in the middle of it."

Placing the water and piece of jaggery in front of the girl, the old woman suddenly shivers – a child sits beside the girl. The child, dripping sweat, looks like so much boiled spinach, wilting in the heat. Anxiously, fussily, the old woman exclaims, "Hurry, put some water on his eyes and mouth!" The girl does so, and then wipes the child's body with the wet anchal of her saree.

The old woman sits at a distance, and stares steadfastly at him. A bouncing, healthy child, no doubt the first offspring of this young, healthy mother – as young and fresh and full of sap as the first shoot of the gourd plant! In the old woman's toothless mouth, under her tongue, a fountain erupts, filled with warm soft saliva.

My, how the child perspires! The water in his body seems to be pouring out! His eyes have turned red! What can she do? Why did they come to her? Why did they come? She would like to grasp the plump child, soft as dough, and clasp him to her skeletal breast! Across her ancient, withered flesh a thrill trembles, her limbs begin to shiver. The sap is oozing from his body, she can all but taste him in her saliva! Like one helpless, she cries out, "I'm eating him, I'm devouring the child! Run, run, take your child and leave!"

The girl, the child's mother, is drinking out of the water pot she held upturned to her face – it slips and falls to the floor. With a startled, pale face she looks at the old woman's wide-eyed gaze – "Is this Ramnagar? You are that...?" She shrieks in fear, snatched up her child and flies like a bird.

Oh what can she do? She feels like tearing open her chest with the nails on her bony fingers, and gouging the greed out of herself. If she

• THE WITCH •

could cut off her tongue, she might find release. Shame, shame, shame! How will she show her face in the village tomorrow? Not that the folks there will have the courage to say anything, that she knows. But how will she face the unspoken accusation in their eyes? As it is children run away when they see her. After today, they will probably fall to the ground unconscious! Oh, the shame!

She remembers clearly how she had fled her village in shame in the dead of night. A girl of her age and caste, Sabitri, had given birth the night before. Everyone had come to see the child. Sabitri had been sitting in the sun with her newborn lying on a quilt beside her. Dark, with shining skin, such a lovely child!

As she had today, so too on that fateful day she had thought how much she would like to take the dough-soft baby, clasp it to her breast, kiss its lips and suck it, devour it. At that time she had not known her own evil powers, she'd thought that this was her desire to love the child.

Sabitri's mother-in-law had come out running, scolding Sabitri, and screaming, "Wretch! Who asked you here? If something happens to my baby I'll teach you a lesson, you'll see!"

She had pointed her finger towards the gate. "Out, get out! Look at the wretch's eyes!"

Meanwhile, Sabitri had picked up her child to her breast, and walked trembling into the house. Deeply wounded, she had come away. Again and again she had thought to herself, shame, shame! Is that really what she was capable of? Even if she was a witch, could she really harm Sabitri's son? Shame, shame! She had called upon God, and asked him to be the judge: "Give Sabitri's son a hundred years' of life, have mercy, prove it how much I love her son!"

But, before the afternoon was over the hungry greed of her

poisonous eye was proved to be cruelly true. Sabitri's son's body had bent like a bow. He had cried out in such pain, it had seemed as if something were sucking the blood from out of his body.

In shame she had fled to the woods near the cremation grounds of the village and hidden herself there. She had spat repeatedly on the ground, to see if indeed there was blood in her mouth. She had even wanted to force herself to vomit, to understand. At first there had been nothing. Then a few drops appeared, and then a quantity of fresh blood. That day she knew without a doubt that she possessed an evil power.

In the middle of the night – it had probably been chaturdasi, yes, it had been – the drums of worship sounded at the goddess's temple in Bakul. The goddess Tara, powerfully alive – every month, before the full moon. There was worship, and the sacrifice of animals. But even the mother goddess had not pitied her. How often had she begged – "Mother, make me a human again, I don't want to be a witch, I will slash my chest and offer you the blood from it." But the Mother had refused to look upon her with compassion.

The old woman sighed deeply, her mind filled with grief. Her thoughts, like kites cut loose, seemed to swing gently and free themselves drifting away to some far off place. The yellow stars in her small eyes gleamed absently. She cast her gaze over Chatiphata. Grey, not a wisp of breeze, the dust covered Chatiphata like a blanket, so smooth it seemed to erase all shapes and forms that lay beneath.

The strangers in town, the girl and her child, had barely left the village and crossed two others when the baby died. He had not stopped perspiring. It appeared as if someone had wrung his life's juices out of him. Who else? That destructress! The girl had beaten her breast and wailed, why had she gone there, why had she gone to the witch? What had she done?

The Witch

The village folks trembled in fear, and desired her death. A band of young men, intent upon punishing her came and gathered at the waterfall near her house. The old witch rose like an enraged cobra and hissed at them: What could she do? Why had the girl come to her? Why had she held out her soft and lovely child in front of her eyes? Suddenly, in the intense anger which assailed her, she shrieked out like a hawk. The young men fled in fear. Today she sits hissing like an angry python, bringing up her rage, then swallowing it. Sometimes she feels like giggling insanely, sometimes she feels like shaking Chatiphata with her screams, and sometimes she feels like tearing out her own hair and rending the world apart in her grief. She feels no hunger today, there is no need to cook anything. Oh, she has just sucked the life juices from a child.

A breeze ripples through the air. The bright light of the waxing moon lies over Chatiphata like a white carpet. Somewhere a restless bird calls out. Crickets sound in the mango grove. It seems as if, behind the house, near the waterfall, two people are speaking in a low murmur. Have those young men come again to cause her harm? Cautiously, with soft steps, the old woman peers around the corner of her house. No, it's not them. It's the Bauri woman, deserted by her husband, and her moon-struck Bauri lover.

The girl is saying, "No, someone will come here, I must leave."

The boy protests, "Who'll come here? No one comes here in the daytime, leave alone at night!"

"Even so. If your father will not let you get together with me, then why should I stay here with you?"

Oh, shame! Where will she go? If these two want to meet in secret, then why here? Why don't they come into the house? Why be embarrassed in front of an old woman like her? What is the boy saying? – "If my parents won't agree to our marriage, let's you and I go to another village and marry. I can't live without you."

Who can speak for his choice! He likes such a fat woman! She remembers, some thirty miles from her village, the betel-leaf seller's shop at Bolpur, with its large mirror. Pictured in the mirror, a tall, slim girl of fourteen or fifteen. A head of thick dry hair, a small forehead, a sharp nose, thin lips. Small eyes, with yellow pupils, ah, but those eyes had beauty! She had been looking at herself in the mirror. She had never seen herself in a mirror before – she had none of her own.

"Who are you? Where did you come from?" a tall, broad young man had asked. She had come to Bolpur just the night before. She had taken shelter there, after Sabitri's son's died on the night of chaturdasi. The man did not appear to be unpleasant, she liked what she saw but she didn't like the way he spoke to her. She had stared unblinkingly at him, and asked, "Why, wherever I come from – what's it to you?"

"What's it to me? I'll throw you to the ground! See my fist?"

Gritting her teeth in rage, she had wished that she could suck the man's blood out of his body. A body like unblemished black stone. The fountain of water ran beneath her tongue. Without reply, glaring at the man, she had come away.

That day, as soon as the sun had set, a huge white-yellow perfectly circular moon, shaped like a plate, had risen in the east. Sitting on the steps leading down to a pond at the edge of Bolpur, she had been eating the puffed rice tied in the anchal of her saree, and staring at the moon. The light of the moon had still not taken on the colour of milk. In the translucent light, everything appeared misty. Suddenly she started as someone came and stood before her. It was the man she had met earlier! He laughed – two dimples showed on his cheeks – and

• THE WITCH •

said, "Why did you run away and not answer my question?"

She had said, "Leave me alone or I'll scream."

"You'll scream? See that slimy pond? I'll throttle you and bury you in it!"

She had been terrified. She had stared helplessly at his face when suddenly the man had stamped his foot violently upon the ground and screamed. She had been startled – the puffed rice she held bundled in her saree had fallen to the ground. How the man had laughed! She had begun to cry. Embarrassed, the man had scolded her for being a cry baby, and had told her to run off.

His voice had even been affectionate.

Crying, she had asked him, "Are you going to beat me?"

"No, no, I won't beat you! I had only asked – where is your home, where are you from? You jumped at me – so I'm saying – "

He began to giggle again.

"My home's far from here, in Patharghata."

"What's your name? What caste are you?"

"My name's Sharadhani, people call me Shara. We are doms."

The man had seemed happy, and said, "Oh, I belong to the Dom caste too. But why did you run away from home?"

Her eyes had filled with tears again, as she had thought to herself, "What shall I say?"

"You ran away in anger, I suppose?"

"No."

"Then?"

"I have no parents, see? Who will feed and clothe me? So I've come here to find work."

A **dom** is a person of an untouchable caste, usually associated with work related to corpses and their cremation.

132

"Why haven't you married?"

She had stared in amazement at the man's face. A witch such as her – who would marry her? She had shivered. Then she had been overcome with shyness.

The old woman, for some unknown reason, begins with bowed head to pick up the dust and stones lying around. The thread that links all these events seems to have slipped – as if, while stringing a garland of flowers, the needle has fallen from her fingers.

Oh, the mosquitoes! Just like bees fall upon someone who has broken their hive, the mosquitoes have fallen upon her. But where are the girl and boy – she cannot hear their voices any more. They must have left. Carefully creeping along the walls of the house the old woman comes out and sits by the door. They will certainly come tomorrow! Where else would they find such a lonely, remote spot? No one for miles around would have the courage to come here. But they would. What can love have to fear!

Suddenly her mind wriggles alive. Well? Would she eat that boy? Such a strong, strapping young body!

At once she trembles and shakes her head. No, no.

A few minutes later, she begins to rock herself. Then she rises, goes to the courtyard and begins to roam around. She needs a way out! She has already devoured a child today, so no sleep for her tonight. She wishes she could cross Chatiphata and go far away. People say, she can ride on trees. It would be good if she could. She could sit on a tree and ride through the sky and the clouds and go wherever she wished. But she would not be able to hear the words of that girl and boy. They will surely come tomorrow.

She giggles. Here they are! The boy sits quietly. He turns his head repeatedly towards the path. She'll come, she will!

· THE WITCH ·

She remembers an incident in her own life. Having wandered around all day, that young man had shown up, as expected, by the pond. He had, in fact, come there before her and was sitting swinging his legs absent-mindedly, watching the path. She had giggled shyly.

"Here you are! I've been waiting so long for you!"

The old woman suddenly starts. Those words, those very words were the ones *he* had uttered. This boy is saying the same words. The girl is standing in front of him; she is probably giggling too.

That day he had brought some food in a packet. Holding it out to her, he had said, "You dropped your puffed rice yesterday. This is for you."

But she could not put out her hand to accept the food from him. The terrible greed in her breast – her witch's mind, like a snake swaying to the snake charmer's pipe, undulated again and again to the music – but it seemed not to know how to strike.

What had she done then? Yes, she remembers. Do these people know, or do they do the same? Oh my! Just the same. The boy is lifting up his palms to the girl's face. The old woman strikes the floor noiselessly with both hands and shakes with silent laughter.

But her laughter comes to a certain and sudden halt. With a deep sigh she quietly sits down with her back to the tree. She remembers how *he* had said to her, right after, "Will you marry me?"

She had not known what to say, what to think. Her ears had grown warm, and sweat had fallen in drops from her body.

He had said, "See, I work at the factory, I get a decent wage. Because I'm a low caste nobody wants to marry me. Will you?"

The young lover, beside the waterfall, said, "Everyone in this village will protest – my caste and family will also, as will yours. Let's run away – we can then live together in peace."

He spoke softly, but in that sequestered, silent place, his words floated clearly to her ears. The old woman remembered with a heartfelt sigh how she had also run away with the young man and, far from those who knew them, had set up house. At the Boiler – so it had been called – at the huge, barrel-like machine – he had stoked coal. He had earned more than the others.

The girl's voice floated in above the sounds of the waterfall. "First tie ten rupees in my saree, then I'll go. What if we can't eat in some foreign land because we don't have the money?"

For shame, the girl needs to be beaten with a broom! Why should she want, with such a strong young man! Ignorant woman! Not silver, but one day she'll see her wedding bracelets bound in gold! Shame!

The boy remained silent. The girl spoke again, "Why, why aren't you doing this? What are you saying? I'm not going to stand here any longer."

The boy sighed sorrowfully and asked, "What can I say? If I had the money, I'd give it to you, I'd even give you silver bracelets – you wouldn't have to ask."

The girl looked scornful, and declared, "Well, I'm leaving then."

"Go."

"Don't call me back."

"Very well."

The white-clad girl seemed to merge with the bright moonlight. The boy sits in silence near the spring. Pity! What will he do now – who knows? Maybe he will become an ascetic, or he'll put a rope around his neck. The old woman trembles. Perhaps she could give the girl the silver bracelets she so wanted? And money? She could not spare ten rupees. She had twenty one. She could give maybe two, at most five out of that to him. Would that be enough? Perhaps the girl

· THE WITCH ·

would not object. Oh, the pity! A time of youth, of happiness, of desire – a pity. She would give the boy the silver bracelets, and the money – like a grandmother to a grandson. She would tease him, and crack sharp jokes!

She approaches the boy and with both hands on the ground bends over him. The boy sits up as if in a trance, unaware of her presence. She cackles and calls out, "Hey, lover, are you listening?"

Hearing her toothless mumble the boy starts up with a shout. And then, he turns and begins to run as fast as he can.

In an instant the old woman experiences an unreasonable change of mood. Like an angry cat, she swells up and hisses, "Die, die – die!" In her arises the simultaneous desire to suck up, on a current of anger, his blood, flesh, fat, marrow, his life's sap, and devour him in an instant.

The boy screams, and crumples to the ground. However, he forces himself up and staggers off.

By afternoon, the next day, the entire village is in shock. That vengeful witch had shot her poisoned arrows at one of the Bauri boys! It was rumoured that the boy had gone to the spring in the evening. The ogress, lusting after human flesh and sap, like a tigress stalking her prey, had crept up on him silently and confronted him. The boy had tried to run, but the ogress had dropped him to the ground with her arrow. A sharp piece of bone, anointed with spells had been let loose – it had sunk deep into his foot. What a rush of blood had spewed from him when this was taken out! Immediately thereafter, the fever had come upon him; and it seemed as if someone, pressing down on his head and feet, bending his body like a bow, was wringing the sap out of him!

But what could she do?

Why did he turn to run? He would run away? He would run

from *her*? Such a strong young man – he could fight with fire – that he should be reduced to a fleshless skeleton of a fish!

An exorcist had been brought in. He had claimed he could make the boy better. But the boy had dried up, died by inches. His ailment – a nagging fever, a cough. But why then had he coughed up blood?

In the silent afternoon, the old woman paces her yard restlessly. In front, Chatiphata smoulders like the ashes of a pyre. No movement disturbs its stillness. Even the breeze is still.

Even he whom she had loved more than life itself, against whom she had never felt an iota of rage, even he had dried up in the heat of her gaze, he had rendered the blood of his body and died in an instant. And some exorcist will protect this boy against her fury, her raging eye!

She laughs shrilly, cruelly. Oh, she is gasping for breath – she can hardly breathe. Such pain – she feels as if her chest will burst – she wants to weep at her suffering. That exorcist is probably trying to bind her in a spell. Try, try your best!

But she will have to flee from here. What a miserable fate she had suffered after her husband's death, after the people of Bolpur had learnt her dreadful secret! She herself had told them the truth. She had been friendly with Sankari, and one day, in her sorrow, confided her secret to her.

After that she had been forced to live on the outskirts of the village, having little to do with the people there. How many places she had been forced to wander! And she was to wander again.

What's this? A shrill cry pierces the sleepy stillness of the fierce afternoon heat. The old woman stiffens, then runs like a crazed person into her room and bars the door. When dusk falls, she ties her belongings into a small bundle and sets forth across Chatiphata. She must flee, she must leave quickly.

THE WITCH

An unusually thick darkness was falling; everything was still, silent. In this silence, the old witch was trying to flee, the dust flying around her feet. After some time, she sits down – she doesn't have the strength to go further.

Suddenly, today, after so long a time, she begins to weep heartbreakingly for the husband that her own evil eye had killed: "Come back, come back to me!"

The northwest portion of the sky had turned tawny, like the pupils of her razor-sharp eye.

In a while, the dust at her feet receded under the whippings of the fierce gale. The old woman too dissolved into it. What a storm! And just a few drops of rain.

The next day, the village folks could not contain their surprise at what they saw dangling from a sharp branch of a thorny tree on the outskirts of Chatiphata. Impaled upon it was the old witch. While travelling through the sky (they said), she had been hit by the exorcist's spell, and, like a bird with an injured wing, had fallen upon that branch and met her death. Beneath the branch a handful of Chatiphata's dust had turned dark. The witch had shed her black blood there.

The serpent venom of old mingled with the witch's blood to make Chatiphata more ominous than ever. It appeared to stretch endlessly, with no hint of direction. A smoky greyness lay like a pall, making earth indistinguishable from sky. In the upper reaches of that greyness something small and black grew gradually in size as it drew nearer.

A flock of vultures was descending on Chatiphata.

"Daini." From *Rahasyer Swad*, ed Subandhu Bhattacharya, Writers Syndicate, Calcutta, 1964.

BANAPHUL
Giribala 8

It was the night of the new moon. Darkness, unbroken, lay thick across the land. Nature itself seemed to tremble with an unnamed dread. A cloudless sky shimmered with stars. These too seemed to quiver. The jackals were setting up a shrill howl from time to time. Then they'd stop, just as suddenly, and the dark stillness would seem to thicken further, only to be shattered by the shrill dirge of night insects. A sound like a lament, heart-broken, despairing. A wind like the last breath bursting from millions of dying breasts, rushing like a storm.

Brihatlal was striding across the field. Many a field had he crossed, even a river bank or two. He had come a long way from the scene of the incident but still did not feel quite at ease. He thought, once across this field and safe at home, and he could be at peace. A powerfully built man, he was garbed in coarse khaddar and a Gandhi topi. The jackals took up their howl again. And abruptly stopped. The shrill sound of the night creatures pierced the dark like an enormous knife.

But the khaddar clad Brihatlal was deaf to these sounds. He could hear nothing. His ears rang instead with cries of, "Oh Ma, Ma, help!

Although the author does not specify the events from which Brihatlal is running, the story appears to be set during the period immediately after the Indian Independence of 1947. This was a time for violent conflict between the landowning classes and the landless and low caste poor in eastern India.

Khaddar or khadi, an indigenously woven cotton material, symbolic of India's national pride against British imperialism.

Save me, save me! They're setting fire to the house, they're burning it down! They've killed my father! They're dragging my mother away by the hair! Don't you dare touch me, don't, don't, don't ..."

Brihatlal, running, reached home at last. He had no one there – he had not married and his parents, brother and sister were dead. All that remained was the house itself, and the temple to Kali with the idol installed by his forefathers. The goddess was believed to be potently alive, and most watchful.

Brihatlal felt like offering obeisance to Mother Kali before he went into the house. The temple doors were open. Had the priest forgotten to shut them? Why was there no light? He stood before the open doors. The darkness inside seemed thicker than the night and more ominous. Suddenly he started, listened intently. Someone seemed to be walking around inside. A dog? A fox? No ... but what was this? Someone was sobbing. A quiet, muffled sound. Brihatlal had a torch in his pocket. He shone it at the altar – and drew back in amazement. The idol was missing, the altar empty. The next moment he shuddered in fear and closed his eyes. Then he felt it must be an illusion ... and cautiously opened his eyes again. But no, this was no illusion – it was Giribala herself. The same Giribala. The same dark skin. The same long tresses down her back. Naked and drenched in blood. Rivers of blood streaming down her thighs. How did Giribala get here? She stood, her hands covering her face.

Kali, the dark and powerful goddess Time, belongs to a group of Shakti goddesses in Hinduism. The word Shakti means force, power, energy. Such deities are associated with the forces of nature and creation, and are therefore, Mother goddesses. The various symbols on the Kali icon are of profound philosophical significance having to do with the cosmological complementarity of male and female, Time, life and death. She has, through Bengal's checkered history, symbolized the Bengali motherland, as well as the power of its women.

"Giribala, Giri ..."

Suddenly, she seemed to merge into the darkness.

Brihatlal turned and torch in hand stood for a few moments – then ran into the house. It was empty, everyone had fled.

"Saudamini ... Mohan ..."

There was no sign of the servants. Brihatlal entered the room quickly and switched on the light. The radio caught his eye. He regretted not having had its broken valve repaired. He could have listened to it to while away the time, even learn about the state of the nation. He stood for a while staring at the radio. A single thought occupied his mind. How did Giribala get here? He thought he had ...

Suddenly the lights went out. Was there trouble at the powerhouse? Or had someone snapped the wires? Brihatlal stood for a while in the dark. For a few moments he did not remember the torch in his pocket. When he did, he shone it and saw that the bed was already made. He lay down on it, closed his eyes, and felt at peace. But the feeling was shortlived.

He leapt up again, and sat on the edge of the bed. He had felt long hair brush against his face. A thick mane of hair. He touched his face but found nothing. It wasn't a cobweb, was it? He lay down again. Again, that touch of hair. He shone his torch and went out to search for a lantern. It took him some time to find it. As he returned to the room with the lighted lamp, it seemed to him that a crowd was streaming in through the open door. As if they had been waiting, and had entered as soon as the door was opened.

"Who ... who are you?"

Silence. Brihatlal entered the room with his lantern.

There was no one inside. He locked the door, lowered the wick and placing the lantern to one side, lay down again. Again, he closed his eyes. Silently, he began to chant the Ram naam mantra. He wanted to sing Mahatma Gandhi's favourite hymn but could not. Every time he opened his mouth a presence seemed to clasp its hand over it. An invisible hand – but he could feel its pressure. He went back to chanting the Ram naam. A harsh grating static disturbed the silence. Brihatlal opened his eyes but could not comprehend anything at first. Then he saw rows and rows of people seated on the floor. Men, women, children – all seemed to be wearing masks, their eyes did not blink, they did not breathe. Brihatlal shuddered to see those who stood behind – a man without arms, two with eyes that hung loose from their sockets, a headless torso, and another, lipless, with his teeth gruesomely exposed ...

That jarring static sound again. Amazed, Brihatlal heard the radio come to life, saw the green light on it now burn a blazing red!

The radio spoke: I am a daughter of Bengal, desperate, unfortunate. No radio station today can broadcast my plea. So I speak through this instrument – I must be heard! Till my death I had thought that this was independent, civilized India. Now I know that to be a lie. Hooligans rule the land – the good are in danger, their life, self-respect, language and culture at dire risk. My father gave up all he owned and embraced poverty to serve his country, my brothers went to jail, one was even hanged for his role in the Swadeshi movement. The independence that we thus won, at such cost – now has no place for us. None at all. We have heard the speeches of great politicians – all false, so much froth, songs stuck in a groove, theatrical playacting. We trust them no longer – our faith lies in ashes. Jinnah Sahab was right – minorities are indeed helpless in independent

• GIRIBALA •

India, crushed by the brute majority into non-existence. We are fated to be refugees – repeatedly. We will be raped by hooligans – again and again, even as our politicians fly around in their planes and shamelessly recite false words of peace. Our self-respect is at stake, we must protect ourselves. Or this scene will be repeated – over and over. I have been raped in the bright light of day, dogs and jackals have torn at my flesh, my loved ones are all dead, my house burnt to ashes. I no longer am a citizen of India – but of the world beyond. But I cannot forget my motherland. I burn with frustration, with grief, indignity and with a desire to avenge. I seek revenge! To punish the lustful demons, the goddess Chandi sacrificed her shame. Naked, with sword in hand, dark as the clouds, she assumed the colours of war. All you women who still live, you too must assume her form – for the sake of your self-respect! Arouse, awaken the goddess who lives in you! She speaks through me today. I can see her hold a newly severed head. I can see the necklace of skulls around her neck, the girdle of corpse-heads at her waist, the god Shiva at her feet. She says to me – "That lascivious lustful animal that sits there, offer him to me in sacrifice!" She gives to me her infallible weapon ...

The radio burst open and a dark arm wielding an enormous gleaming falchion emerged from within. The next moment Brihatlal screamed. And everything fell silent. The lights went out, the radio stopped.

Brihatlal's body was discovered in his room the next morning. His head was not to be found. It was assumed that the jackals or even dogs had dragged it away. But later a more fearsome discovery put the lie to this assumption. The priest had gone to pray at the Kali temple in Brihatlal's house. He ran out to give the news.

Brihatlal's head had been found. All the people rushed to the temple and found his severed head clasped in the goddess' hand, the stone head that hung there now on the floor.

"Giribala." From *Rahasyer Swad*, ed Subandhu Bhattacharya, Writers Syndicate, Calcutta, 1964.

SWAPANBURO

Nightcall 9

When Jhanta was a little baby his mother fell dreadfully ill. So he was raised by Ahhladi pishi, a distant cousin of his father's, who had never been married, being slightly off in the head. And, with reason or without, because she said things as they came to her, everyone called her "Ahhladi." So to the children in the household she was Ahhladi pishi. Ever since his mother's illness, when she had first pulled Jhanta on to her lap, he had grown so attached to her that even after his mother recovered, Ahhladi could not let him go. Jhanta too was devoted to his aunt. She would have to bathe him, feed him, dress him and tuck him into bed. He could not do without his aunt for a moment. On her part, Jhanta's mother, busy with the many demands of a large household, was relieved to leave her son with Ahhladi.

Ahhladi pishi loved to eat fish. Especially shol, a freshwater fish. When Jhanta grew a little older he would catch all kinds of fish and bring them home for his aunt. She would laugh in delight and say, "Thank my stars my Jhanta's here, I can have a little rice and fish now and then!"

In the monsoon, when the rivers and creeks, filled to the brim, would spill over on to the land, and the family pond would be full to bursting, Jhanta would be up at dead of night catching various kinds of fish with his polo, the pail shaped wicker basket used for catching fish. And if he landed a shol for his aunt, his joy would know no bounds.

Although Ahhladi pishi lived with Jhanta's father she had some allowance of her own. She guarded her wealth fiercely, spending it only to buy sweetmeats for Jhanta. Jhanta's mother would tease her, "Thakurjhi, don't squander your money away like this!"

Ahhladi pishi would reply crossly, "It's my money, I'll do what I please with it. I'll throw it on the streets if I like, how does it matter to anybody!"

She would proudly declare to everyone that when she died, Jhanta would be the one to perform her last rites at Gaya.

Then Ahhladi pishi died suddenly of a three-day fever.

A hale and hearty woman ... never a day's illness in her life ... no one in the household had imagined that she would die thus, all of a sudden. And the usually wild and naughty Jhanta seemed to have been struck dumb with the touch of a wand. He spoke to no one, refused to eat and sat desolately, staring fixedly ahead. He seemed to wither with each passing day.

Jhanta's mother grew increasingly concerned at this state of affairs. The family brought in exorcists and tied charms and amulets to Jhanta, but all in vain. It was as if the lifeblood was being sucked out of him. The family was beside itself with worry.

Suddenly one night, Jhanta woke from deep sleep with a start.

His mother asked, "Why, Jhanta, why did you sit up in bed? It's still dark. Go back to sleep!"

Jhanta stared blankly about him, then whispered to his mother, "Ahhladi pishima called out to me!"

His mother shivered in fear when she heard this. She stroked her son's head, caressed him, and prayed, "Ram, Ram!"

Thakurjhi is a term used by a wife for her husband's female cousin.
Ram is one of the incarnations of the god Vishnu who protects and preserves life.

• NIGHTCALL •

The women of the neighbourhood warned her, "Jhanta's mother, keep a sharp eye on the boy. That shameless Ahhladi died but really didn't. That's why she's still roaming about!"

A shaora tree stood by the pond near Jhanta's house. The villagers, on their way back home from the haat with their groceries, claimed they had seen someone sitting in its branches.

Brindaban Ganguli had once apparently come face to face with the entity. He said, "Luckily I had the presence of mind to hold on to my sacred thread and chant the Gayatri mantra, or I'd have had my neck broken and been left to die near the creek that flows into Jhanta's family pond!" Such rumour did its whispered rounds in the village. Some believed it, others laughed it off.

It was the month of Ashar, and the monsoon rains had filled the rivers and ditches to the brim. The dark waters swirled across the land, drowning the rice fields. They had run over the banks making a muddy slush of the village paths and had entered the creek that drained into Jhanta's pond.

It was around midnight. The half-light of the moon now revealed now concealed the shadowy contours of the landscape. A thin fog, woven through with moonlight, lay like a pall over the village.

Jhanta was sleeping soundly beside his mother. A black cat yowled horribly as it went around the back of the house. Somewhere an owl screeched annoyingly on and on. A drowsy, heavy stillness hung in the air ... Suddenly it seemed to Jhanta as if

---

The folk belief is that ghosts of various kinds live on trees, and kill passers-by by breaking their necks. Chanting a mantra, or prayer, and/or holding onto the **sacred thread** (here worn by Ganguli, of high brahman caste), is believed to protect against harm.

Ahhladi pishi was calling him from outside the room. She was saying, "Oh, Jhanta, come quick – there's fresh water in your pond. There are so many fish, just come and see! Mind you, don't forget your polo!"

Suddenly Jhanta awoke and sat up in bed with a start. He looked around and found everyone fast asleep. His mother's right arm lay around him. He gently moved it away.

Ahhladi pishi had asked him to get his polo. Jhanta entered the adjoining room in a trance and carefully picked up the polo, then opened the door and crept outside.

Someone seemed to whisper in his ear, "Shut the door, Jhanta, or they'll wake up." Jhanta shut the door without protest and went off with quick strides towards the pond.

The darkest hour of night ... not a soul awake ... rain water gurgling its way into the creek ... Jhanta thrust his polo again and again into the water and hauled in heaps of fish. Where did so many shol come from? Jhanta couldn't fathom what was happening. The khaloi that he had brought with him was full of fish. A charred smell assailed his nostrils. What was it that drew Jhanta so that he crept on with his fish-filled basket? But wait! This was the same shaora tree!

"Will you get me some charred shol fish, Jhanta?"

Amazed, Jhanta saw someone sitting in the branches of the tree. Was it not Ahhladi pishi? It looked just like her ...

At last Jhanta seemed to return to his senses. Ahhladi pishi was dead, after all. Then at whose call had he ventured out in the middle of the night to catch fish? His hair stood on end with fear. He tried his best to make a dash for it but his legs refused to move. He managed, finally, to pull himself together and desperately began to run. He could hear Ahhladi pishi's nasal voice crying after him, "Oh Jhanta, please leave the shol fish for me, I don't want anything else."

The more she called, the faster he ran. Suddenly a long arm stretched out of the shaora tree and snatched the khaloi of fish from him. Jhanta screamed and fell down in a dead faint. When the people of the household heard his shriek and rushed out to see what the matter was, they found him foaming at the mouth. Finally, three days later, after his mother had cried her heart out, Jhanta opened his eyes. But he remembered nothing of what had happened and could only stare blankly around.

The villagers said, "Look here Jhanta's mother, from now on you'll have to watch him every moment. The petnis call people out at night just like this, break their necks and then leave them to die near the swamp."

Jhanta's mother's blood froze when she heard this. She stayed awake at her son's side all night long, sighing and fretting and lamenting, "What has happened to my peaceful home? At what inauspicious moment did I offer shelter to another's daughter?"

About this time the household suddenly noticed that there was a crazed look in Jhanta's eyes. Suddenly he declared, "I'd like some charred shol fish."

And at once a charred shol fell into the centre of the room. Everyone started in fear.

Gradually the whole situation became easier. Whenever Jhanta would want something, it would immediately appear before him! One afternoon, weak and tortured by the heat, Jhanta said, "Ma, give me a glass of cold water."

No sooner had he spoken than a beautiful glass of crystal clear water appeared out of the blue. Jhanta was about to drink it, when his mother dashed it to the floor crying, "Don't touch that Jhanta ... the petnis are getting these for you!"

The women of the village would come in groups every evening to see Jhanta. Somewhere in the middle of all the whispered speculation, Ganguli's wife declared, "I am out of chewing tobacco! I don't like tobacco that's not from Kashi."

Absent-mindedly Jhanta asked, "Do you want tobacco from Kashi, Thandi?" And at once a box of tobacco fell on the floor!

Ganguli's wife cried in amazement, "Why, here's tobacco from Kashi! A new box! Where did it come from, Jhanta's mother?"

Those who were there, and knew how things were, explained it to her.

Ganguli's wife had been about to pick up the box but when she heard about Ahhladi petni, she cried "Ram, Ram" and headed straight home.

There were frequent incidents like this. All of a sudden the house would fill with the fragrance of champa flowers. Immediately after, the stink of rotting fish would send people running helter-skelter, holding their noses. Once, the village boys were heckling Jhanta, when, all of a sudden, they began to be pelted by bricks. But the funny thing was, not one fell on Jhanta. The bricks rained down on the boys' backs and heads like the fruit of the palm tree in the month of Bhadra. Shouting and screaming they frantically escaped in all directions.

As long as these events were entertaining, people gathered in crowds. They sat around, agog, waiting for the petni to perform her tricks. But for how long could they stay up nights and go without sleep?

Gradually the crowds began to thin ... the bustling house fell empty and eerily silent again.

Bhadra is the fifth month of the Bengali calendar, from the middle of August to the middle of September.

• NIGHTCALL •

One night Jhanta's mother was woken by a nightmare. She clutched her son to her bosom with all her might. From the back of the bamboo shrubs where the crickets chirp relentlessly, a wailing strain could be heard.

Startled, she sat up. Placing her hand on her son's forehead she prayed all night to the goddess Durga. She felt that someone was trying to snatch her child away from her.

It had been drizzling continuously since the evening. In the distant forest, the foxes howled out at regular intervals. It seemed as if they too were in the grip of some unnamed fear. The birds had huddled into their nests much earlier that day. The cows were lowing in their sheds and it seemed as if they had had a foreboding of the ominous. Occasionally, the screech of the black owl floated over the land.

A strong wind cleaved the village, blowing northwards from the cremation grounds towards the marshy lands ... as if a petni were sighing! Not a soul walked the village paths that night. Not a child could be heard crying. Every living soul seemed to be counting the hours to some dreadful calamity in breathless terror.

What death-like sleep enveloped all those in Jhanta's house! The stove had not been lit that evening. The maid who had gone to put the coals and cowdung cakes into it, had fallen asleep right there. The men of the household, who sat around the chessboard all evening, and whose shouts kept people awake for miles around, had today set aside their game at evenfall and were now snoring on the rug.

It was raining relentlessly. The frogs in the ponds kept up their chorus in rhythm with the sound of the rain. Dark clouds covered

---

The Orion or **Kalpurush** is, in Hindu myth, the attendant of Yama, the god of Death.

every star in the sky. The Kalpurush seemed to hang suspended over the earth, holding his breath, awaiting the impending disaster. In the roar of the storm, a hint of the ominous ...

Lying next to his mother, Jhanta was sleeping soundly. So soundly that there seemed to be no life in him.

The relentless rain, the raging storm, the cry of the crickets, the chorus of the frogs, the screech of the owls, and the silent suggestions of the Kalpurush, seemed to have lulled him into that sleep from where there is no waking up.

But suddenly a voice whispered from the fence. "Jhanta, wake up, come here. The ponds are brimming over with fish tonight."

Jhanta woke up at once, alert.

That insistent whispering call came floating to him again.

Jhanta sat up with a desolate look in his eyes. Who was it – where was he supposed to go – he did not know – but he stood up, like one possessed.

Again that call ... like whispers in the bamboo grove ... luring him, "Don't bring the polo with you today, Jhanta, bring the net this time ... and come out quickly with me ..."

He could not resist this enigmatic call of the night.

Jhanta picked up his fishing net and slung it across his shoulder. He unbolted the door and stepped out into the yard.

Immediately, a deafening clap of thunder ... and the furious flapping of bats' wings ...

But even the thunder roused no one.

Following the beckoning hand of a shadowy figure Jhanta proceeded towards the water.

The darkness lay deep around the path, yet he found his way with ease.

"There, there it is! Look at the fish beating against the banks! Can you see them, Jhanta? Go on, throw out your net."

At that disembodied command Jhanta walked right into the water.

And sank without a trace among the leaves of the hyacinth. No one in the entire village had even an inkling of what had happened!

Only the black cat yowled and paced restlessly near Jhanta's mother. She did not wake up from her deathly sleep.

When the fishermen pulled out Jhanta's body in their net the next day, the whole village recoiled in horror.

An elderly village woman smote her forehead and cried, "Ahhladi became a petni, but still couldn't forget Jhanta – so, like Rahu, she pulled him on to her lap!"

Years have passed, but the villagers still fear to go near the water late at night. They can hear someone crying there, running about and beating her breast with her hair blowing wild in the wind.

"Nishirdak." From *Bhuter Galpo*, ed Indrajit Ray, SriPrakasbhavan, Calcutta, 1967.

LILA MAJUMDAR

Chimaera 10

I was not always this plump and housewifely. Before he married me I used to be a large-eyed slim young damsel. And this thin-as-a-rat's-tail braid, now twisted severely into a tiny bun, once flowed like a serpent, black and smoothly glossy. But inspite of my dusky beauty, enchantment was yet to touch my staid existence. I remember clearly, how day followed monotonous day. The colours of the rainbow seemed to pass me by. I would not eat much, or sit at ease, or speak too loudly, in case I became too complacent to snatch at such delights that might come my way. Such sacrifice proved useless – those rare days of my dull youth flowed past unfettered as a clear brook. One day I woke up to find that I had turned the last pages of my youth.

I was furious at this realization. The reams of poetry that I had written in my mind, the wonderful and improbable events I had created in my imagination, were these to come to nothing? The wondrous, the extraordinary, that which would always secretly beckon to me and then vanish, would it always give me the slip? I was very angry. I yelled at him: "You annoy me. Night and day you have a smile stuck on your face. You are losing hair from the top of your head. You have become fat. You snore at night. You don't call me your Queen Bee any more. My life is wasted!"

He gave me an astonished stare, and went back to his shave.

Suddenly one day, quite unexpectedly, this wasted futile life of mine brimmed over with mystery and magic.

We moved into an old house. Everyone moves house in the

morning but we moved in just before twilight. The sun had not yet set but its waning light was turning red. The ash-grey outer walls of the house, the dark, deep green of the mango and grapefruit trees that surrounded it, where a flock of birds nested, were tinged with the colours of the setting sun. I had heard of the utter loneliness that is the human lot from birth to death, a loneliness that nothing whatsoever may dispel. I felt this relentless solitude in my soul ease a little in that instant.

The wooden steps in the old house were no longer carpeted though marks remained of shining metal rods which had once held a thick red carpet in place on every step. The ground floor had been refurbished in a modern style. But the rooms upstairs, above the carpetless stairs, belonged to some bygone age. Those unseen presences, who had vacated this house for us for a brief while, would return again to fill every nook and cranny when we left. It has taken me some time to say all this, but the moment I stepped into the house, these thoughts shot through my mind like lightning!

The house was filled with the magic of old things. All the furniture on the ground floor was new. But even after meticulous cleaning, the rooms above, with their ancient worn-out furniture, beckoned to me night and day. Perhaps there was really nothing there. The ancient university of Nalanda, the empty temples of Bodhgaya too had aroused in me this curious sense of déjà vu, this feeling of sharing an intimate relationship. As if, if I thought a bit deeper, I would be reminded of matters of great significance. But alas, this present life of mine – a gift from my mother in this birth – passed it by. And here too, the many rows of broken upper windows stared, unblinking and inscrutable, at the mango and grapefruit trees, and that which they should have revealed, remained unsaid.

• CHIMAERA •

Perhaps as a child I had inadvertently partaken of some magical potion, the intoxication of which still remained in my eyes and in my blood. I would feel that more than half my life is over, yet that which is of prime significance, beside which all else pales, that seems to have altogether passed me by. I would wonder, why in my youth did I wait expectantly all night to see what marvel the morning would bring. And all day wait impatiently for the night – would it yield to me its dark delights, its hint of things not of this world? Why did the play of light and dark upon the leaves, the shimmer of moonlight, and the golden tremor of sunlight seem so tinged with mystery, so inviting?

One afternoon I sat pondering over all my shattered dreams. The servants had cleaned the kitchen and left to smoke their bidis somewhere in the shade. The children had gone to school, he was at work. I was alone. The morning sun had lost its glare. The pickled olives and green chillies that had been set out in the veranda were no longer getting its heat. I put these away. I brought in the washing and let the dog off its leash. Then I went upstairs, to the room in the north, where I had stacked my old magazines, to look for Pramatha babu's story about a wonderful couple.

The magical enchantment of old things lurks even in a clutter of old magazines, in anything that was once so contemporary and useful, but now has gathered the dust of neglect. In that still afternoon I sank under the spell of that dust. But suddenly, alert, I looked up and saw her.

In that instant I lost my sense of the probable and the improbable, my faculty for rational thought – so I was unafraid. I gazed at her in wonder. She stood at the door, bending a little, looking into the room. My gratified eyes drank in her serene beauty. I admired her from her lotus-like feet from which the decorative red aalta had faded to her black-bordered country-style saree, her white blouse, her short flowing curls, her flawlessly beautiful pale face, her hands adorned merely by a pair of bangles, gathered at her breast. In one hand she held a small enamelled brass box, worked in blue and green, in the other a long necklace of green stones. Beautiful. Like the verdant depths of a forest in the monsoons; like a smooth stream of rain that reflects the dark shades of the trees; like the crystal clear waters of a lake green with the shadows of the trees, in the heart of a deep forest. I took in the breathtaking beauty of that necklace and listened, mesmerized, to the gentle clink of its beads.

She had not seen me. Her eyes were intent upon something inside the room. Following her gaze, I too looked inside to see what it was she sought so intently, so eagerly, in that empty room. I turned back to the empty room and saw only the door-frame with its missing door, and peeling paint. She was gone. I was thrilled to the core. For the first time in a youth lost to monotony, a dull middle-age, I felt the thrill of the extraordinary. I forgot all about Pramatha babu's wonderful couple and distractedly made my way downstairs. Whenever I closed my eyes I could visualize again the fall and sway of the deep green necklace in her flower-like hands.

I did not want to talk about this incident to anyone. I forgot my usual effusiveness and kept it a secret. After that day I went upstairs many a time for many a chore and waited, but did not see her. Eventually, her image grew misty and unclear in my mind. I even suspected that I had, in fact, dreamt the whole thing. At a point when almost all thoughts of her had left me, I saw her again. This time too it was during a still afternoon in the autumn, in the busy rustle of dry leaves in the breeze.

The man who used to buy back my old newspapers had not come

for a while, and I had taken a bundle of the month's newspapers upstairs to store. Placing these at the foot of the broken dressing table, I straightened, and saw her – so close I could have stretched out my arm and touched her. Each time that I saw her, I saw her all of a sudden, complete, whole – I did not see her come and go, nor did she materialize slowly before my eyes. I saw her in her entirety. In amazement I beheld the faded red aalta on her feet, her black-bordered saree, her loose curls, her pale and beautiful face, the graceful hands gathered at her breast, and in them, the enamelled box. I looked more closely today and saw the blue-green Chinese dragons with red eyes that adorned it. I saw too the long necklace of large green stones that she held, deep-hued as the dark green bamboo leaves reflected on the still waters of a moss-covered pond and the shade of the drooping willow on its shores.

Staring, I saw again that shadow of an unfulfilled longing, some deep discontent upon her face. The darkened stars of her eyes seemed transfixed on a single spot. Following her gaze, I saw today an expensive blue carpet in the room that had been empty for so long. On the carpet, strewn carelessly, were hundreds of paintings, oils done by a deft hand. I saw too, one on an easel, near the window, lighting the room with that now familiar pale and beautiful face, that same black-bordered saree and loose hair. And the necklace of green stones. I saw the artist as well, albeit unclearly, for my own eyes were misted over as I trembled with unaccustomed emotion. Leaning on that broken dressing table, holding reason at bay, I watched amazed the tall figure of the artist. I saw through a blur his clothes and ornaments, his fair complexion, his close, tight-lipped mouth, his arched eyebrows and piercing eyes. I saw everything, but hazily. In fact, I conjectured more than I saw. It seemed that the artist was past his youth, but was not into middle age either. On his face I saw a peculiar detachment.

My senses were as if under a spell, only my faculty of sight remained. My enchanted reason accepted whatever my hungry eyes fed upon, in silence, unquestioning, without suspicion.

The artist, paintbrush in hand, waited as the woman silently went and stood before him, facing the light. I did not see her walk from the doorway to the interior of the room. One instant she was near me, so close I could smell the sweet fragrance of her hair, hear the soft tinkle of the beads in her trembling hands. The next, I saw her as she stood facing the easel. There was no exchange of words. Her thirsty eyes seemed fixed in profound expectation upon the artist's face but his gaze remained absorbed and indifferent. It was as if I was not present, as if I was unseen to them, as if this material body, this restless consciousness, this curious gaze simply did not exist. I saw him draw with a deft hand, stroke upon brushstroke, with exquisite confidence, downcast eyes on his busy hand, while her doting eyes moved from his face for not even a moment. A deep silence pervaded the room.

I do not know how long I remained like that. Suddenly I noticed that it was getting late, the shadows of the trees lengthening in the light of the setting sun. I looked outside the window for an instant. When I looked back the otherworldly occupants of the room had vanished from sight. I felt weary. Standing immobile at the dressing table had numbed my limbs, and my eyes closed in exhaustion.

The winter passed, as always, with its age-old chills. I could not speak of what I had seen to anybody. It seemed that on the one hand, my life had always been full, my husband, my children, my friends, my many duties – these remained as they were. But that which in me had never found expression, the hope which had begun to give way to despair, now secretly hummed with excitement, blossomed like a garden. My old and secret sorrows, my private discontents, paled into insignificance. Now it seemed that the walls which had hemmed in my world had collapsed, that I was as free as the sky, as the breeze. I felt – I can't put it in words, how can I say what I felt then?

I saw her for the last time in February. The air was redolent with the fragrance of the blossoms of the mango and grapefruit trees. The touch of spring was upon every leaf, and flakes of old paint drifted down from the rooms above. That evening I thought I saw a light upstairs. I climbed the stairs slowly, my heart pounding like a hammer. I stood quietly at the door, as silently as if I was the apparition. I saw her leaning against the dressing table, looking around the room sorrowfully, with a clay lamp raised in one hand, holding in her other the green stone necklace. In that dim light its colours captivated me.

An empty room, with a blue carpet, and an empty easel. The scattered paintings had been gathered carefully and stacked against the wall. The room looked unused.

I was watching her sympathetically when she suddenly looked at me. She could see me, I was no longer invisible to her! I realized this with quick delight. She made a delicate gesture of offering, stretching out her hands bearing the necklace to me. I could not bear the deep despondency in her eyes. She appeared to search my eyes for compassion. I put out my arms to embrace her. I had the sensation of being immersed in water cold as the morning dew. I felt its chill on my eyes, in my heart. She flowed through the binding circle of my arms and mingled with the breeze. And yet I distinctly felt, as she left, that she had offered me her necklace. I felt its cold hardness in my hands. For the first, and last time in my life, I fell down in a faint.

They returned from the playing fields, the office, their friends' homes. Not finding me, they came upstairs and carried me down.

They splashed my head with water, and fanned me, and I regained consciousness. To escape their questions I hid my face in my pillow and pretended to be very tired.

Late that night he said, "I have a lovely gift for you, and you choose this day to give us such a scare!"

I remained silent.

He continued, "Some old things were being auctioned off in the hall near the courthouse. Look, I bought this necklace for you. There was an enamelled box with dragons on it, but the Collector's wife bought it for a large sum."

Wide-eyed in wonder I saw, draped loosely on his hand, a necklace with large green stone beads, as dark and lovely as the grapefruit tree in a shower of rain.

"Sonali Rupali." From *Sab Bhuture,* Ananda Publishers Ltd, Calcutta, 1983; 1989.

KAMAKSHIPRASAD CHATTOPADHYAY

The Lady of the House 11

The middle-aged woman who answered the knock on the door was wearing a saree with turmeric stains on it. She had a strange look in her eyes. "Are you here to look after Ginnima, my dear?" she asked Malina. "I've just put the vegetables to cook. Come in. You have my blessings. May you return home safe and sound," she said.

Malina was a little nonplussed. She had come to work as an ayah. So why would she not be able to return home safely and why did the woman bless her – she really could not understand.

Perhaps the woman was slightly crazy. She talked to herself. Malina heard her muttering under her breath as she returned to the kitchen, "Another young thing ... so many have I seen come to grief ... Narayan, Narayan, may the girl live ... such a lovely face ... like that daughter of mine ... Narayan, Narayan ... may the girl ..."

She abruptly turned back to her work when Malina entered the kitchen.

As she fried the vegetables she warned: "Be very careful. See to it that nothing falls on the plate. If anything goes wrong Ginnima will throw a fit."

As she stood outside the closed door of Ginnima's room on the first floor with a food tray in her hands, Malina's heart beat uneasily. Her arms and legs tingled – why she couldn't say. She had, after all, been working as an ayah for almost five years now. Started right after

---

[1] **Ginnima** is a term for the senior woman in a household.

marrying Milan, in fact. They needed the extra income. But she'd never felt this way before. She'd always prided herself on the fact that she wasn't a person who was scared easily. So what was the matter with her today? Malina was cross with herself.

She pushed open the door carefully with her knee and stepped into the room.

A shutter of the south-facing window overlooking the street lay open. The other windows were closed, leaving the room in a half-light. The bed was about an arm's length away from the open window. Ginnima lay on three pillows piled one upon the other. It was winter, and she was covered in a quilt that left only her hands and face visible. Her covered form loomed like a mountain. Her arms were huge — more like an elephant's legs. It was impossible to say how many layers of fat had accumulated in her heavily sagging cheeks. There seemed to be no bones beneath those quivering layers of flab. Her eyes, however, were extremely piercing. Malina's heart froze when they met hers. They were the eyes of a snake! She had never seen such a cruel gaze, such an obese body.

She had heard that Ginnima suffered a paralytic stroke nearly fifty five years ago. Not having walked in all these years she had given way to corpulence. Malina had never imagined that she would ever have to come face to face with someone like this.

Fixing Malina with her beady eyes, Ginnima spoke in resounding tones, "So you are the new wench come to work as an ayah? Well, well. Put the tray down on the side table. Come closer. Let me take a good look at you."

Malina set down the tray and stood near the bed. Those eyes made her head reel. She felt as if a current was passing through her body. As if she was drowning. And her body was melting. It seemed as if the room did not exist, neither did the bed, the chair, the table or the cupboard. Nor did Ginnima. All that existed were those beady eyes and a terrifying merciless stare. And nothing else ...

But this lasted just a few moments. Slowly the room, and its furniture came back into focus, as well as Ginnima's huge presence.

Ginnima was speaking with her eyes closed: "You look very young. Not more than twenty two or three. Strong and buxom too. You are no beauty though. When I was your age I was as lovely as a fairy. With luxurious hair, a complexion like butter. Slim and svelte. My waist was not thick like yours. If you only knew how many men's heads I used to turn! How many desperate youths would wait about, wanting to profess their love to me ... but today? In bed for fifty five years. I haven't stepped on the floor for fifty five years. But I haven't forgotten those days when I was a beauty, when I was desirable, when I was young."

But Malina did not feel a jot of compassion for Ginnima after listening to her. Her body did not feel numb anymore. Instead a dreadful throbbing had begun to make itself felt inside her head. As if the centre of her head were beating against her ears. Malina wanted to rush out of the room to the relative safety of the woman in the kitchen downstairs.

Suddenly Ginnima's tone of voice changed as she said, "Here, young woman, why are you standing about? Prop up the pillows. How do you think I'm going to eat?"

Malina was arranging the pillows when Ginnima suddenly grabbed her wrist. Who would have imagined such strength in those fleshy, flabby hands? A cunning smile played on Ginnima's lips. With her other hand she began to stroke Malina's arm from shoulder to elbow. Then she lightly pinched her.

Ginnima spoke all the while she stroked Malina's arm: "You thought I was a fat old woman? Not at all. I am not satisfied merely with food. I haven't forgotten those days of my youth. The languorous luxury of love that made me tremble with pleasure. Did you think that simply because you're young you could have it all for yourself? You have sindoor in the parting of your hair. So of course you are married. Is your husband alive? Talk to me about him. Is the boy tall? Is he strong? How strong? Does he make love to you everyday? How often? Is he muscular? Tell me, tell me. How does he make love to you – *how does he make love to you?*"

Desperately Malina snatched her hand away and immediately Ginnima's voice fell silent. Her eyes closed. Then, looking with blank eyes at the tray, she extended a flabby hand.

When Malina reached the kitchen she was trembling. She felt nauseated. What a disgusting mind! What a filthy person! She felt like smashing everything around her.

Furiously, she dipped into a bucket and started pouring mugs of water over both her arms.

The woman looked at her in surprise and said, "Have you already fallen out with Ginnima, my dear? Of course, I agree that getting on with her isn't easy. But you have to put up with a lot when you work in someone else's house. So think again before you go. So many young girls have I seen come and go as ayahs. Not one can stick it out. I might as well tell you the truth. In all this time, after that last girl who fled due to Ginnima's temper in the month of Sraban – today is the new moon night of Magh – I haven't been able to get anyone to work

---

Magh is the tenth month of the Bengali calendar, from the middle of January to the middle of February.

· The Lady Of The House ·

here. I've worked myself to the bone over the last few months. For a while I had employed two middle-aged women like myself. Ginnima drove them away. Such women are anathema to her. She wants young women. Tell me where do I get them from? And the way young women are today! Within a few days they come out of Ginnima's room and begin to mimic her. They pay no attention to me! They wave their hands about just like Ginnima, they look around with her sharp little eyes and roll them this way and that. One even imitated the exact tone of her voice. My hair stood on end and the blood froze in my chest when I heard this. She was about your age. She lasted about a month. Then one day, at dawn, she hung herself from the mango tree in the garden. No one knows to this day why she did it. It was a dreadful incident. The police were all over the place. They could find nothing."

Malina's eyes were by then streaming with tears. The middle-aged woman glanced at her worriedly: "Don't cry, my dear, don't cry. She's old. Can she be right in the head? She's senile. Does she think before she speaks? Don't pay any attention to her. Keep working, don't say a word. But mind you, my dear ... don't mimic her behind her back like those uppity girls ..."

As the day wore on, the pain in Malina's head grew more intense. She began to grow absent-minded and made mistakes at every step. She cut her thumb while slicing the onions. The bowl of chutney slipped from her hand and smashed to pieces.

"You seem to have lost control of your limbs. Where is your mind? With your husband?" The middle-aged woman remarked glumly.

Malina arranged Ginnima's lunch on the tray and took it up. Her limbs trembled, her throat felt dry and her head hurt horribly. But Ginnima did not even turn to look at her, nor did she say a word.

Malina returned to the kitchen. She washed the dishes, her hands shaking. She managed somehow to eat a little and wondered when it would be seven thirty. When would her husband get off work? When would he finish his job at the factory and come to pick her up on his scooter? Her head felt as if it was being torn apart ... Milan, Milan, when will you be here? Milan ... Milan ...

By the time Malina took the dinner tray from the middle-aged woman and entered Ginnima's room she had made up her mind. If Ginnima so much as touched her and said those filthy words again, she would not take it lying down. She would rip apart that flabby face with her nails. Gouge out those cruel serpent eyes.

What was the matter with her? She had never had such thoughts before. And her head – it had never hurt so badly either.

Surprisingly, this time too Ginnima did not bother to look at her. She didn't say a word. Malina returned to the kitchen and rinsed out the utensils. Then she washed her face and taking out the sindoor box from her worn-out purse, wore a large, red, round mark on her forehead.

Just then the muted honk of Milan's scooter was heard outside. He travelled by scooter to and from the factory and they had decided that he would honk outside the house on his way back. And then they would return together with Malina riding pillion.

Just then the middle-aged woman returned from Ginnima's room and said to her, "Go and meet Ginnima before you leave, my dear. She wants you to. Your husband is here, I see. I'll ask him to wait for a couple of minutes."

Looking helplessly at her Malina went upstairs.

In a voice drenched in honey Ginnima said, "Your husband's here, is he? I can see him through the window impatiently sounding the horn."

Malina replied, "Yes, Ginnima."

"Good, good. Of course you must go home, my dear, sitting behind your husband, holding him closely. I won't keep you any longer. Now I shall sleep. Before you leave, please remove one of the pillows from under my head," said Ginnima in the same honeyed voice.

Malina should have been on her guard then. She should have fled from the room. She should not have placed herself within reach of those destructive hands. But she was misled by Ginnima's honey-soaked voice.

As Malina bent to draw out a pillow from under Ginnima's head, she struck out like lightning at Malina's wrist, grasped it with her pincer-like hand and pulled her close.

Malina's throat was as dry as a bone. Her head hurt unbearably. And Ginnima, hissing like a snake, continued, "No, my girl, you won't be going home, holding your husband tightly to you. You will never make trembling love to that youthful man of yours any more. And he will never know the difference! How will that hunk of a husband of yours come to know that you are no longer Malina, *how will he know?* He'll think his youthful wife has become even more desirable! How happy he will be ...!"

It seemed as if it was not Ginnima who was speaking. But those merciless snake-like eyes of hers. Gradually the dim light in the room grew even dimmer. Those evil eyes became pitch black, like the interior of a coal mine. Dark and deep. Then the two eyes merged into the night of the new moon. And Malina began to drown in them, to drown ...

The room was very still.

Malina's head did not hurt any more. A drowsy dullness suffused her body. It spread to her thighs, her legs, her ankles. How thick her legs had become! They were spread beneath the quilt. There was no sensation in either.

Malina observed herself as she arose from the bed. She arranged her saree tightly around her waist, and draped the anchal over her shoulders. She smiled with suppressed glee at her reflection in the large mirror, and opening the door, left the room. Then she heard her sandalled feet flapping down the stairs.

For the first time she realized that she had not walked for fifty five years. That she would never walk again in all her life.

Her hands began to grow restless. How amazing – how strong her hands were! She looked through the window – and saw herself on the pillion of the scooter, clasping Milan. She heard him ask, "What took you so long?"

She heard her own voice. "Ginnima had called me to arrange her pillows."

"Ginni-ma." From *Nirbachita Bhuter Galpo*, ed Ranjit Chattopadhyay, Ananda Publishers Private Ltd, Calcutta, 1992.

SHISHIR LAHIRI
Wedding Night 12

Sudha knows that after I died and became a ghost I took up residence in the skylight above our room.

This is not breaking news, this is a matter of some six months past. Returning from work one day, I slipped and fell trying to board a crowded bus with a tiger painted on it. The rear wheel made my head one with the earth. Had I not had an ID card in my pocket, people would have taken me to the morgue and dumped me there – an unidentified corpse. But that didn't happen. When, at midnight, the local police broke the news to her, Sudha collapsed like a felled plantain tree.

I was watching Sudha from the skylight in amazement. My wife, Srimati Sudharani Devi – who'd have guessed she loved me so much? What fool then, caught in the wiles of Manju Adhikari, would have run to board that bus anyway?

Even that morning, as I was leaving for work, Sudha, in affectionate farewell, reminded me in sharp and grating tones that if I didn't return on time that evening I would have her to reckon with. Work gives over at five as usual but it's nine o'clock before I get home. "I don't know," she said, "If that typist wench is leading you around by the nose. Today this movie, tomorrow that restaurant … The wife you married stays home, gasping for breath, and you go gadding about

---

At a Bengali wedding the marriage is consummated two days after the actual ceremony. The bed of the bridal couple is decorated with fresh flowers. "Bed of Flowers" is another way of saying **"wedding night."**

178

with some Miss Hoity-Toity. Aren't you ashamed, you brazen man?"

I can't blame Sudha. She wasn't wrong. But she was exaggerating excessively. Manju has a special kind of attractiveness. When, every evening after office, Manju would bat the lashes of her painted eyes, flash a dimple with a smile playing on her lips, and call out seductively, "Debuda, just a minute!" I would be beside myself. How that minute would expand to become two or three hours, I never knew. Of course, at the end of every tryst, my pocket would be somewhat lighter. But who worried about that. Who cared!

Sudha always guessed right. She had caught on to this too. One day, having gone to get my salary, Jaminida startled me. He said, "Debu Mittir, you cannot get your salary." Annoyed, I said, "If *I* can't get my salary, will *you*? Know this, I am the true son of a kayastha, I don't simply hiss. I bite when I have to." Jaminida said, "Then go home and bite your wife. She has presented a petition. Our benevolent managing director has read it, and desiring to keep the happiness, peace, and harmony in your family, has ordered that for you to get your salary Srimati Sudharani Mittir's presence is mandatory."

There was a great to-do at home that night. It did not actually end in fisticuffs but neither of us had dinner, and we went to bed with our backs to one another, clasping our side-pillows in a huff. Neither of us remembered that day that we needed to smell each other before we could sleep at night.

There is such a thing as honour in the office, and I had lost it. With honour lost, so was Manju. Had she come to me and said, "Debuda, I am responsible for this, please forgive me," I might have been saved. But Manju dropped me promptly and took up with a chap close to her own age, draping herself around the shoulders of Nirupam Jowardar, the artist. The callow youths in my department sniggered

· WEDDING NIGHT ·

every time I went by. That creep, Ajay Dasgupta, even said, "Some typing that piece of baggage is going to do! Adhikari's not going to let you put your fingers on *her* keyboard any more!"

I was becoming quite depressed. The fights with Sudha at home, not a moment's peace outside, and the pressure at work – I was absolutely spent. One evening after work I watched angrily as Manju and Nirupam clambered on to the bus, jostling shoulders. I thought, I'll settle accounts with one of those two today. But who was to know that the Lord of Death had sent one of his messengers out after *me*? Trying to leap on to the bus, I slipped and fell. The rear wheel flattened my head like a slate. I died and became a ghost.

Three days later, upon seeing Jaminida from the office, Sudha burst into sobs. "Jamini babu, what about his salary for this month? His pension, his gratuity?"

Jaminida said, "It'll be there, it'll be there. You have been made the nominee, what's to worry? But, you understand, it will take a little time."

Wiping her eyes, Sudha asked, "But how am I to manage, Jamini babu?"

"That's what I'm worried about." Looking concerned Jaminida asked, "Tell me, are you a college graduate? If you are a graduate, then something can be arranged for you. You can find work at the office on compassionate grounds."

Sudha pouted. "Had I been a graduate would I have married that ape? My father pulled the wool over his eyes!"

Hearing the truth, finally, after five years of married life, I was delighted. Laughter bubbled up noisily in me. How was I to know that the sound of my laughter would burst forth like a gurgling fountain? Startled, Jaminida asked, "Who laughed?"

Sudha was listening intently, her head cocked to one side. Rolling her eyes she said, "Who do you think is laughing? It's your Debu Mittir. It's a death by accident, after all. It wasn't enough that he plagued me when alive. Now he's here to plague me after death."

Jaminida paled. Clicking his fingers in front of his face, he said, "I must leave now."

"Don't forget what's owed to me or I'll send the ghost to your house. You'll recognize him by that laugh," Sudha said.

I was beginning to enjoy myself. I laughed again – nasally this time. Jaminida leaped up. Outside the door he made the sign of the cross on his chest, and mouthed a "Ram, Ram!"

When a calf grows new horns, it bloodies them by rubbing its head against a tree. I was most impressed by my own new-found powers. All this time, damn it, I'd been such a wimp. Fearful of Sudha at home; of others outside it. But now I cared a hoot! No one could see me! I leapt off the skylight. I rattled the doors and windows of the house like a storm. I was seized by the urge to shake the two-ton antique bed that had been in my family for two generations. As soon as I put my wish to work, the bed, like an enraged elephant, turned around and rammed into the wall-closet. A few items of glassware fell off it and smashed to pieces.

Sudha ran into the room. Her eyes were swollen with crying, her untied hair looked scruffy and unoiled. When had she last oiled her hair, how dry her skin was! The new saree she wore was rough with starch, and kept falling off. Her eyes burnt with rage. Tucking her anchal into her waist Sudha rolled her eyes and declared, "See, I have enough

---

Sudha refers to a traditional belief where a premature or **accidental death** results in a dissatisfied and malevolent spirit who finds it difficult to leave the world.

Wedding Night

problems of my own, I don't want to deal with your tricks. You've been a clumsy oaf all your life and you're still the same. Aren't you ashamed? Put everything back exactly where it was. Sweep up the broken glass. If you slip up anywhere at all, you'll have me to deal with."

Sudha's grim expression induced a wave of fear in me. One never knew with her – she could call the carpenter and get the skylight sealed. If she got *really* mad, she could call in the Kalinga hymn singers and they would sing so, round the clock, that the sound of the cymbals and drums would force me to emigrate. Or, if she lit a couple of cowdung cakes and smoked me out, would I be able to stay? So, like an obedient child, I cleaned up the house, put the bed back where it belonged and went back to the skylight. I could have died of shame. I hadn't been able to stand up to Sudha when I was alive, and I couldn't now even when I was dead. Oh well, name one husband who ever won out against his wife. You can put the pressure on anyone else in the world, but not on your wife. To them we are all snakes without venom.

I didn't have much strength during the day – my body seemed like a wet cloth – and as soon as the sun rose, I would fall asleep. It was in the evenings that I woke up and as the darkness gathered, would come joyously into my own. Then my body would acquire the strength of a rogue elephant – I couldn't think what to do next. Is it any wonder that people call us ghosts? On some days, when Sudha lay in bed scratching her prickly heat, I would feel like leaping down and lying beside her. But I knew her temper and never found the courage to do it.

Her temper was justified, of course. I had, after all, taken premature leave of my earthly existence. Poor thing, all the worries of life, its awesome responsibilities, had fallen upon her lonely shoulders. Concerned about her new unattached, widow status, her maternal and paternal aunts had descended on her, setting up a virtual police station in the house. But they could get nowhere with Sudha. Within three days she had packed them off, declaring, "I will deal with my own problems. If you come back here to plague me, I will hang myself."

I quite liked hearing this. If Sudha hung herself, then I would not have to be alone. The two of us could have some royal times in this room. I pondered this further and realized I was being unrealistic. Who leaves the living to join the dead? Had Sudha died and I lived, would I have given up everything and roamed about like an ascetic? Or would I, like Manju, have simply found someone else and tried to have some fun? Damn it, the living have a completely different logic. Who cares to understand the tragedy of being a ghost!

One day I observed Sudha sitting by the open window, contemplating the sky. The clouds were gathering darkly, there were flashes of lightning. I was afraid. If it rained too heavily, I would dissolve into the skylight. Even as a child I had always been prone to colds and coughs, and when I caught a chill I would often suffer from fever. If I got a fever now, who would look after me? No one to caress my brow gently, to talk lovingly to me. If I asked Sudha, she was hardly likely to comply!

I was quite absorbed in my worries. Just then I heard a sob. Startled, I looked down and saw Sudha standing by my photograph and tearily saying, "What a witless man, you could find no other time to die. See how hard it is raining outside. On such a day when have I slept without using you as my side-pillow? At my age, tell me, who likes to sleep alone? Do you think I'm not scared? If the thunder's loud, whom will I hold on to?"

My heart burst with compassion. Poor thing! She had just turned thirty, or if my revered father-in-law had lied, thirty two. Her youth

· WEDDING NIGHT ·

stretched ahead like an endless afternoon, such a long life facing her, and I'd selfishly come away alone. Oh, what would Sudha do? My eyes filled with tears at her plight. I said silently, Sudha, do not fear, you won't have to live alone. I will lie next to you. You can make me your side-pillow whenever you wish, I won't say a thing. Sleep in peace all night, I will watch over you.

Sudha sighed deeply and rolled over onto the bed. Bare-bodied. Her saree draped loosely over her breasts. My eyes glittered. I realized the tragedy of what it meant to be a ghost. But I couldn't bring my heart to accept it. I wormed my way through the fine holes of the mosquito net and lay down beside Sudha.

Sudha lay with her eyes closed. Feeling the touch of the cool breeze that I had created, she exclaimed, "Ah! What relief! It soothes me so!" I felt like laughing in joy. But I didn't want to announce my presence just then. Let some time pass, when Sudha's heart is quite soothed, then I would announce, "I have arrived."

Sudha turned slowly to her side. She was looking for the side-pillow. In a flash I transformed myself into a pillow-like support for Sudha's left leg. Sudha's closed eyes sprang open. She stared in amazement. Her leg was not upon the bed, yet it felt as if it rested on a pillow. She sat up quickly. Then furiously she said, "Shame! Shame! You've no peace even in death. Still the same thing! Aren't you ashamed, you low-life? Go. Go, to your camel-faced wench. You can dance in paradise with her!"

I shrank to a speck at Sudha's fury. It doesn't pay to be good to people. The one you steal for is the one who calls you a thief! Sudha railed on. "Your ancestors were low-lives! Now I'll have to set you right. One of these days I'll be angry enough to go perform your last rites at Gaya, and *then* your pranks will come to an end."

Rites at Gaya! Tears flooded my eyes. What will I have left, if my ghostly existence is terminated?

For some days I remained quite depressed. Have I no dignity just because I am a ghost? I had no desire to eat, my mouth felt dry. Nothing pleased me. I thought, I'll become an ascetic. What is the point in going on when one's wife is disinterested in one's existence? Of course, that is, if Sudha was technically still my wife. Are there connubial relations after death, or are these, like in divorce, severed?

After some three or four days of such thoughts, I grew angry. My extremities felt shaky, restless. Suddenly I thought, for whom do I suffer thus? My head flattened by a bus, and now dying afresh under the weight of Sudha's curses, while that luscious career woman, Manju, with her made-up eyes and dimpled cheeks, giggled and carried on with Nirupam. It was unbearable. I had to teach them a lesson. I die. And she has fun. This cannot be, must not be.

To get my body in shape I began to exercise seriously – doing push-ups inside the skylight. I swelled the biceps of my arms, the muscles of my legs. After some time, when I felt I was in form, I spread out my arms and took off, scaring an itinerant bat or two, sending them shrieking in fright into a lighted room. In the distance an owl hooted.

I had not considered the possibility that there were owls in Calcutta. Now I thought that the city's inhabitants, living in their tiny apartments, had become owls themselves. You couldn't find them in the light of day. When the night grew bright with city lights, then they flew off in pairs. No food cooked at home, they ate at some restaurant or other. When the night deepened, they rolled into bed.

Leaving Curzon Park, I arrived at Maidan Market. Manju had

Wedding Night

bought herself quite a wardrobe of sarees here with my money. I passed by the movie theaters. How many movies we had seen together! Manju preferred films with a lot of sex and violence so she could cling to me in fright, or pull my hand on to her lap and play with it in a way that made Sudha seem as colourless as a clay doll in comparison. At those times I had felt Manju is my life, Sudha my death. But in the end, everything turned out quite the opposite. I died because of Manju. And Sudha tried so hard to save me, but couldn't.

I flew to Manju's apartment building. The door of Apartment Number 77 was, as expected, closed. A blue light lit the room. Peering through the keyhole, I saw two people in the room, and some sort of liquid on the centre table. It had been such a long time since I had sipped that liquid. My mouth watered just seeing the glass.

I leapt up. Gliding through the skylight, I stopped short in surprise. This was not Nirupam, this was Ajay Dasgupta! Manju had changed partners once again! I thought, Encore! Well done! You, Manju, you who change men like your clothes, you will be Queen Cleopatra some day!

Ajay was lying with his head on Manju's lap. His salt-and-pepper French beard smelt of liquor. His arms encircled Manju's neck and he was pulling her to his face, trying to say something.

I felt like laughing. Bastard, one day you hooted at me. I'll teach you a lesson today. I slipped like a fly between Ajay's fingers and pinched Manju hard. Manju jumped up in surprise to her feet and cried, "You idiot, why did you pinch me?"

Trying not to fall off the couch, Ajay exclaimed, "Me?"

Manju's back was inflamed – quite red and swollen. It was a ghost's pinch, so this was to be expected. Manju said, "Who could it be, if not you! Is there someone else in the room!"

Ajay looked at his hands. Manicured nails. They were not sharp enough to deliver such a pinch. He spread out his hands before her and said, "You tell me, can I pinch you with these nails?"

Manju was snorting in fury. Pulling her anchal back on to her shoulder she huffed, "I don't want to see anything. You're drunk. Leave me alone! You heard me! Get out of here!"

Ajay was aghast. "Is this a joke? You've just spent three hundred rupees of mine, and I'm to get out?"

He reached for the glass of liquor. I raised the glass some eight inches above the table. His eyes widened. He cried, "What is this? The glass is flying, it's floating in the air!"

Manju was staring, fascinated. Her mascaraed lashes did not even blink. I raised the glass some more and poured it over Manju's head. Then, raising the bottle and drinking its contents in one quick gulp, I emitted a shrill laugh.

Manju and Ajay yelped in fear and fell to the floor, clinging together in fright.

I laughed so hard, I threw up.

It took two days for my disgraceful hangover to wear off. I spent these two days squeezed, willy nilly, into Manju's apartment skylight. Just as it's impossible to sleep well in a strange bed, the same was true here too. But what could I do, I had no choice. I could not leave until I had recovered. What if I fell and broke an arm or leg, I would be a sight!

After Manju had left her apartment early that morning, she had not returned. She refused to enter it. For no other reason than, that like everyone else, she feared for her life.

On the third day I returned to my own skylight. I noticed that in just two days my room appeared different. There were new curtains

Wedding Night

on the windows, a Kotki cover was spread on the bed, each pillow wore a newly-frilled pillowcase. The room had been swept clean of all cobwebs. Even the tailless gecko that frequented our room was no longer around. A garland of flowers adorned my photograph. Incense sticks burned in the five-pronged holder.

What was the occasion? What was happening? Was I being honoured today? Had Sudha finally got the money from my pension and gratuity? She should have got it by now. It was going on six months. That was it. I descended from the skylight and fingering the garland that adorned my photograph thought, Why, Debu Mittir, how do you feel today all dressed up like a bridegroom? You didn't merit a garland when you were alive, you just digested the curses, and now, having died you look rather grand. Long may you live, live in bliss, in joy.

I heard a door being opened and leapt up to my skylight. Sudha entered. With her was a large and prosperous man. Over six feet tall, with a military haircut. His biceps swelled through the sleeves of his tight-fitting shirt. His shoes squeakily announced their newness. A shiny revolver hung from his belt.

I stared in amazement. I hadn't seen this piece of work before. Who the hell was he? Sudha was laughing, "I can't any more, Rajatda! You made me laugh so in the cab all the way here, even now I feel giggly."

Rajat replied, "Why shouldn't I make you laugh! I come here to find you sitting around with a dour face. As if there's nothing to live for, no joy in your life. I say, man must die. Just because your husband's dead, you don't have to fall apart – I've never seen anyone else act this way. Look at the state your house was in. It's looking quite presentable now, in these two days. I won't let you stay here, you know, I'll take you with me to Dehra Dun."

Twisting her saree around a finger, Sudha said, "How can that be! What are you saying!"

Rajat said, "I know what I'm saying. The day your maternal cousin Sanat told me about you, my heart said, you must be protected. How can you live like this? When your money runs out what will you do? Oh, life is long, and you're so young! I will get you married off. And if I can't find anyone else, then I'll marry you myself. I am, after all, a confirmed bachelor. You won't mind garlanding one such."

As soon as he finished speaking, Rajat roared with laughter. Hearing him, I thought, this fellow is like the Amjad of *Sholay*. What a laugh, like a victory-drum beat, pounding in one's chest.

So I figured: Fine, very convenient. Sudha's heart is broken and who the hell are you? I never saw you around when I was alive. I don't know who you are. Take off the shine, let me see who you are.

Sudha had grown thoughtful at Rajat's words. Presently she said "Let me think a little about it, all right? This is such a huge step!"

Rajat said, "Of course you must think about it. Think as much as you want. Ghosts act thoughtlessly, not humans. Think before you act — that is what humans do."

The mention of a ghost probably reminded Sudha of me. Looking at my photograph she asked, "Rajatda, do you believe in ghosts?"

Rajat, again emitting that bone-shattering laugh, said, "Ghosts, ghosts are in the mind. If I were a believer in ghosts, I'd be dead. How many battles I have fought, how many men I have killed. If all of them became ghosts and attacked me, would I have lived? I'd have kicked the bucket long ago."

Sudha's eyes widened. "You don't believe in ghosts. But I can show

---

This is a reference to the villain of a very popular Hindi film, *Sholay*.

WEDDING NIGHT

you a ghost. I have a tame ghost right here. Whatever I ask, he obeys. Shall I call him? Do you wish to see him?"

Rajat sprawled his legs out further on the settee and suppressing his laughter asked, "Is this ghost on a leash, or will he bite like a monkey?" Then in a loud voice he said, "Well, call him. Let me see your Mister Ghost."

I was burning with rage. I thought, I'd like to teach him a lesson. Not that I'd do much – If I simply tugged his tie this way and that his tongue would stick out a mile. But again, I thought, Sudha's attitude doesn't seem favourable. She doesn't seem decided about which way to turn. If, yielding to Sudha's command I presented my self to Rajat, the consequences could be disastrous rather than otherwise. Besides, there was the question of my dignity. Just recently I had suffered such indignities trying to be helpful – Sudha had threatened to lay me to rest once and for all by going to Gaya! What did I need such trouble for? I was a ghost now. *You're* human, be the way *you* should be. There's no love lost between ghosts and humans.

"Oh, my dear, do you hear me, would you come just this once?" Sudha called out lovingly.

I kept my mouth shut with great difficulty.

Sudha pleaded, "Laugh again, won't you?" Then she said, "Fine, if you don't feel like laughing, move the couch a bit. Then I'll know that you're here."

Sudha's loving words, her pleading, tickled my fancy. But I remained steadfast and tucking my neck into my shoulders, bit hard on the skylight and stayed put. It had been five years since I'd heard such soft words from Sudha. Does such a stubborn woman forget so quickly? Had she spoken to me this way when I'd been alive, then Debu Mittir would not have been suspended from the skylight at that moment.

190

Sudha's Rajatda looked around briefly, then guffawed. "Not only God, even ghosts fear the military man. Your ghost was here, but he's run off in fear. Come to me, listen."

His long arm came to rest on Sudha's shoulders. I closed my eyes in alarm. I couldn't bear to look any more. A woman should protect her own chastity – that isn't the job of a ghost.

About three days later Sudha came home dressed as a new bride. I watched with increasing amazement. Who would have said she'd lost her husband only six months ago? The Chinese hairdresser had dressed her hair in a stylish coiffure. A bright red Banarasi saree draped her body. Her face appeared to glow. Her eyes, lips and face made-up, like Manju. Her body looking quite trim, her youth bursting from every pore. Well, well! How fine she looks! I had never seen her looking like this. She seemed like a second edition of Manju to me.

Rajat entered the room carrying a bouquet of flowers. Today he had on a cotton panjabi and a pleated dhuti. Ornamental sandals adorned his feet. Presenting Sudha with the flowers, he said, "Decorate the bed with these. This is our wedding night." Then, looking around him, he continued, "Why have you hung that over there, Sudha?"

"What?" Sudha raised her eyes.

"There, that picture of your late husband."

"Where else should I put it?"

"Wherever!" Rajat abruptly pulled my picture off the wall and shoved it under table with his foot. Then he said, "Nothing from your past should come between us, Sudha. From now on, you are mine and I am yours. No one called Debu Mittir ever existed. That's all."

Oh, wonder! What words! Debu Mittir becomes no more than an illusion! The man is crafty, I must say. What a commanding tone of

• Wedding Night •

voice. He now behaved towards Sudha not as an older brother, but as a husband! I shook myself and sat up. I had needed some time to know what was going on and now was ready to act.

Someone rattled the door knob outside. Food was being delivered from a hotel. Rajat took the food and closed the door. Then, laying the table, he asked, "Are you done? I'm hungry."

Goodness, what a variety of dishes Rajat had laid out! From chicken biryani and fried fish to pudding. Fried fish used to be my favourite dish. Once, when I had eaten twenty one pieces of fried fish at Brajenda's daughter's wedding, Sudha had lovingly called me a ravenous ogre. Oh! Those days were gone!

Having arranged the flowers on the bed, Sudha, with sparkling eyes, sat herself down at the table. Pulling a flat bottle from his pocket Rajat drew two glasses to him. Then, pouring a peg and downing it neat, he mixed about half of a peg of lime juice with the liquor and pushed it towards Sudha.

The gin flowed freely, I saw. No, I had no time today to indulge these desires. Booze will send me under the table faster than I know it. I could still feel that creep's foot kicking at my photograph. I must punish him. For a moment I considered entering the battlefield. Then I thought, Slow down, Debu Mittir, slow down, let's see what happens.

Sudha, picking up the glass, said, "Liquor!"

Rajat draped his left arm around her shoulders. "Yes, my sweet girl, today we will celebrate. After such a long time I feel that I have achieved something. A real piece of good work."

Sudha, rolling the liquor around in the glass, said, "But I don't drink."

Rajat looked up at her. "If you didn't, now you will. At least today let's have fun. Anyway, that's not liquor, that's wine. Wine and wife go together. Love is no fun if we're not drunk."

He roared with laughter. Sudha held her nose, took a sip, and asked, "Couldn't we postpone things a bit? Until we've been to the Registrar's." For shame! The wedding night before the wedding, I feel uncomfortable thinking about it."

Rajat glared at her. Biting on a cutlet, he said, "What are you saying? Where the Mother Kali is a witness, is that not a marriage? Look, I asked a priest to put vermilion in the parting of your hair. It's a real marriage."

Sudha said, "That wasn't a real priest who married us. Who knows if he's a brahman or not!"

Rajat poured himself another peg. "Don't worry about such things," he said. "I have very little time, and a lot of work. I've given the notice at the Registrar's office – when they call us, we'll show up with our witnesses and put our signatures where required. I've let the bank know, tomorrow my account will be made joint with yours. I have to make you my nominee on my insurance policy."

Sudha asked, "How much money do you have in the bank?"

"Oh, about two lakhs or so. The insurance is for a lakh."

Sudha looked very uncomfortable. She lifted a spoonful of biryani to her mouth. Rajat looked at her and said, "I can't stay here much longer, I have to leave for Dehra Dun. Before I leave, I'll sell your house. That money, and whatever little you have can be put in the joint account." Looking at Sudha's face a while, he continued, "If you want you can open another account for yourself."

Mother Kali refers to the goddess "Time." Marriages which cross conventional or social lines are often performed at her temple, where she serves as "witness." Traditionally, vermilion powder applied to the parting of the bride's hair proclaims her new status of wife.

•WEDDING NIGHT•

Now I understood what all this was about. All that stuff about Sudha's cousin, Sanat, was a lie. Rajat had got wind of her recent condition from some place or other. This was a con man. He was sure to destroy Sudha. I felt sorry for her. Oh, but she really wanted to get married. Who wants to remain the wife of a ghost?

I began to giggle. Rajat turned around and asked, "Who's laughing?"

The colour returned to Sudha's face. She replied, "My husband."

Rajat ground his teeth. "I'm your husband," he said.

I leapt down and said, "Who do you think you're fooling? Is it enough just to change one husband for another? It'd be something if there had been a real wedding. I would be able to say nothing if you'd put your signatures at the Marriage Bureau. You're making a show of marriage and trying to make a grab for my house, my money and my wife!"

Rajat grabbed Sudha with one arm. Taking out his revolver with the other he cried, "I'm a military man, I won't have any problems blowing away a wimpy ghost like you!"

Sudha was trembling with fear. I said, "Neither you nor your forefathers were ever in the military. You're a fake, through and through!"

Sudha screamed, "Save me!"

I quickly pulled Rajat's dhuti loose. Trying to hold it up, he loosened his grip on Sudha, who sprang on to the bed. Rajat too sprang upon the bed and shouted out, "No one's going to come between me and what's mine! Your ghostly husband won't either!"

Sudha screamed out again. I homed in on Rajat like an arrow and bit him on the nose. As he jumped up, Sudha ran for the door. Rajat, in blind rage, let loose his revolver.

I became nervous at the sound of the gun. That tiger-marked bus had made a similar sound when it ground my head like flattened rice.

Leaping up to my skylight, I saw Sudha already seated there, dressed in red. Swinging her legs cheekily, she said, "You're really clever, aren't you? You'd thought you'd leave me by myself and have fun with Manju? Wait and see, now I'll have the ring in your nose."

I said, "You're no less yourself. Where is your handsome Rajat? Is there to be no wedding night then?"

Sudha laughed. So did I. After that, dear readers of both sexes, I can say no more. I'm too shy to say any more. For shame! Our two unadorned bodies, the he-ghost and the she-ghost, gradually merged and became one. Our spectral voices joined together in joyous harmony. Our wedding night had arrived with the promise of an unexpected spring.

"Phulsajya." From *Nirbachita Bhuter Galpo*, ed Ranjit Chattopadhyay, Ananda Publishers Pvt Ltd, Calcutta, 1992.

MAHASWETA DEVI

In the Forests of Jharowa

13

To this day Mainu, Sonam and Tata are not sure if their experience in the forests of Jharowa was real, unreal or simply a dream. Yet it is true that the four of them had entered the forest. And, that Badal had not returned ever.

It was at Badal's insistence that they had gone to Jharowa. Otherwise they had never even heard of the place. Badal's uncle was a timber contractor in a forest at Palamau. Badal was to start work with him that year. The four young men were close friends since their school days. Mainu and Tata had just begun work in a bank. Sonam was to join his father's newspaper office soon.

Badal had always been restless and impulsive. His constitution too was robust. In fact, he did not look like a Bengali at all. Inspired by him, the four of them had toured India on bicycle. They had even scaled the Himalayan mountains a few times.

Badal had an amazing ability. A few instances would illustrate this.

They had once explored the path of a glacier at Gangotri with the Young Men's Club. When they decided to set up base camp, Badal had protested at their choice of location, saying, "Not here. There will be a dreadful calamity at this place."

The party's leader, Mohanbabu, was furious. He was an experienced mountaineer. With him were three skilled sherpas. Did they know better, or did Badal?

Even so, Badal was insistent and took his friends back to the tent. That very night, as the moonlight bathed the snowy slopes, an unexpected landslide wiped out Mohanbabu's base camp completely.

A similar thing happened on a visit to the Taj Mahal at Agra. All of a sudden Badal said, "We must leave this place right away. Something is going to happen and we will get involved if we stay."

Right next to them a young man sat motionless, staring fixedly at the Taj Mahal. No one seemed as absorbed in it as he was.

They came away. Apparently, just half an hour later, two men opened fire on the youth. The latter was armed too, but was killed in the ensuing skirmish. A few bystanders were injured.

Badal could sense impending calamity. Mainu, Sonam and Tata had seen it for themselves. What happened then in Jharowa?

It all seems like a nightmare.

Badal was to start work in March. He was very excited. He could roam through the forests, and have all kinds of thrilling experiences. It was he who said, "Why don't you come too? You can stay for a few days, then return home."

"Can we go hunting?" they asked.

"Oh," he replied, "Hunting's prohibited. But you can shoot birds."

"And maybe a deer or two ..."

"Where shall we stay?"

"At my uncle's bungalow. Kaka's not married. He's spent his entire life in one forest or another. At one time he used to capture elephants in Burma. Let's go, he'll regale us with his stories."

Kaka had chosen quite a place to live in – one had to first get off the train at a forest station called Komandi, then travel another forty miles by jeep into the interior and finally reach a place named Suma. The Suma river meandered by, dancing over the pebbles. A high barbed wire fence surrounded his house.

At one time work had begun to mine bauxite here. This had gone on for several years. Then, for some reason, the mines had been closed down. The roads that had been built for the mines were still there. Trucks carrying timber plied these roads to Daltongunj.

Kaka, they discovered, was a man of few words.

"Why have you used barbed wire fencing, Kaka?"

"Because of the elephants."

"Can they not dig up the fence?"

"They can, but they don't. They are very intelligent."

Even in March it was chilly in the afternoon, and cold as evening set in.

They ate a dinner of roasted wild partridge and chapatis. Kaka seemed to be in a better mood after coffee.

"You've come here, but things are not going well," he said. "Work is at a standstill in the best forest. I don't know what will happen."

"Why? Why has the work stopped?" they asked.

"I don't know, I cannot figure it out myself," he replied.

"Do tell us, please," they implored.

"On that mountain," Kaka began, "Is the forest of Jharowa. It is a virgin forest, rich in sal trees."

He told us the story. A Punjabi gentleman had taken the forest on lease. But for a strange reason – he wished to live in solitude.

He built a house there, and brought home a wife. It was heard that they had even had a child. Each week Dhillon used to come to the market for groceries.

Suddenly, for a few weeks, there was no sign of him.

Then, one day, a horrifying piece of news reached Kaka. Dhillon's jeep had been found abandoned by the roadside. His corpse lay in the house. His wife and child were missing.

Kaka went there to see for himself. He found Dhillon lying on the veranda. On his face and in his eyes was an expression of utter terror.

Inside the room lay their huge Great Dane. There was not a drop of blood in either. Dhillon's corpse was as white as a sheet of paper.

There was no trace of his wife and child.

The body lay in the open in that sprawling house. No hyenas or jackals had torn at it.

Kaka's jungle coolies were convinced, "This is the deed of some evil spirit."

And it was from them that Kaka learnt more. Dhillon had married a girl of whose antecedents he knew nothing. Finding her wandering alone in the forest he had brought her home and married her. Would a human girl roam about alone in such a dense forest?

Kaka had paid no heed to these stories. If you must work in the forest you cannot be a coward. And he knew that the coolies believed strongly in spirits and ghosts, in demons and monsters. He had Dhillon cremated, and the dog buried. He returned in his jeep after locking up the house.

Then, through the Forestry office, he inquired about Dhillon's family. Finally, a young man named Verma arrived from Ranchi. Dhillon was his maternal uncle. Verma said, "I shall not live in the bungalow. I'll simply load whatever there is in the house into the jeep and return to Ranchi."

A friend had accompanied Verma. No jungle coolie went with them, and they spoke their minds clearly. "We don't fear animals," they said. "But who would venture into a place where even animals do not dare?"

Kaka scolded the head coolie whose name was Dasain Oraon. The coolie said, "Babu! We will not go there at all. Tell the other Babu that he shouldn't be going either."

Verma scoffed at these words. It was from him that Kaka took the forest on lease. A virgin forest with huge sal trees – each would sell at an excellent price. On the day that Verma was to leave, Kaka met him at the market. Verma said, "Do drop by tomorrow morning. And if you can make some tea and get it along, there's nothing like it."

That was the last time they met. The next day, when Kaka took a thermos of tea and arrived at the forest, he found both Verma and his friend lying on the floor. Both dead, eyes wide open in terror, their bodies drained of blood.

"And then?" asked the boys.

"Both had small puncture marks on their throats."

"What could that mean?"

"I don't know. The police are still investigating. They have no leads yet but a terrible fear has been unleashed. No one goes there now to fell trees."

"Not even the police?"

"They've been there a few times. There too lies a mystery."

"What do you mean?"

"The police lock up the house each time they leave. But when they return, it is find it open. Everything in place, spick and span. Who would say that no one dwells there?"

"What do you make of it?"

"There is some human agency behind this. That is what I believe. A thousand and seventy sal trees, karam trees, tamarind trees ... it's a forest worth hundreds of thousands of rupees. Someone is initiating this fear."

Kaka seemed rather depressed. He had relied greatly upon the Jharowa forest.

Badal said, "Why are you so worried? There are four of us, we'll stay there taking our rifles with us. All these mysteries will be cleared up."

The next day Dasain Oraon took them to the Chipa Forest. Trees were being felled there. Dasain was a dignified and serious man. He wore a cotton vest and shorts and held a stick in his hand. He said, "Don't go to Jharowa."

"Why? What's the matter with the place?" they asked.

"Sit down, let me explain. Hey you, get some tea."

Next to the overseer's tent a man was brewing tea in a kettle and selling bidis. They sat down on a felled tree. Dasain said, "Babu understands quite a lot. But not all of it."

When they had heard it in the forest, Dasain's story had seemed to be just that – a story. But today, in the city, it rang true to Mainu, Tata and Sonam. How was this possible?

The story goes like this –

"In the beginning, long long ago, when the earth was being created, the demons' wives fought a battle with the great god. God then hurled the wives down from the sky. They became the mountains. And from their wombs, over time, grew forests. But soon after, all kinds of men have taken over possession of the forests and the land.

"Even then, some parts of the forest remain protected. Since men are taking over everything, the spirits of the mountains and the forests stay perpetually displeased with them as they are being forced to leave their rightful home. So they take up certain places as their abode.

"The forest of Jharowa is such a place. But Babu pays no heed to this fact, he just does not understand. He has never stopped to wonder why, in the place where Dhillon built his house, no birds sit in the trees, and no animals roam about. Dhillon, too, had never stopped to ask how a girl came to be in the forest – and he even married her. Of course, he could hardly have done anything else. The moment he made his home there, he was as good as dead. By the time he saw the girl, he was already under the spell.

"She was no human, but a spirit. In a bid to take revenge on mankind, it goes out to entrap men, at times in the guise of a girl, at times as a deer or a peacock. It then sucks the blood out of the men and leaves them lying there."

"Why?" asked Sonam.

"And why not? Aren't the men felling trees, quarrying stones out of the mountains and sucking the lifeblood of the forests?"

"I hope nothing has happened to you folks?"

Dasain laughed a lovely, gentle laugh. "We are not the ones killing the forest, Babu," he said. "We are not destroying the forests and hills to make money. Why should they kill us? We are the sons of the forest. We follow the rules of the forest gods. They are angry at the men who come from outside. It happens like this – we are walking through the forest. Suddenly a branch snaps and falls in our path. But there is no wind, no breeze, so why did the branch fall? At once we know that we are being warned. We do not venture any further and turn back."

Tata asked, "Who keeps the house clean?"

"The one who has had **Dhillon**, that's who."

"Why?"

"They want to eat more, they want more men."

"Why did they not do anything to the police?"

"Who knows!"

The fact that nothing had happened to the police convinced Mainu and his friends that this was all the doing of some human hand. That was when Badal decided that they would go to Dhillon's bungalow.

Kaka asked them not to go.

The police officer cautioned them too.

Had they, instead, actually asked them to go, the boys' enthusiasm would have vanished. But as a result of all the warning, what had so far been mere enthusiasm, now became stubborn determination. Four strong young men. They swam, rode motorbikes, and were skilled mountaineers. They had joined the Rifle Club together and all of them knew how to use a gun. Badal even had a license. He had acquired one before starting his job in the forest. Mainu had learnt karate, and Tata and Sonam, judo.

The police officer Suja Singh said, "Fine. I'll stay on today in Suma, this side of the mountain. It's been a while since we've played a good game of cards."

He stayed on in Kaka's bungalow. And as the boys left in the evening, he told them over and over, "Sound carries far in these lonely mountains. Keep this whistle with you. Blow on it if there is danger and we'll be there."

Dasain accompanied them for some distance, then returned, shaking his head and muttering to himself.

A small hill stood midway between Suma and Jharowa. The road to Jharowa wound up round and round along its side. When they arrived at Dhillon's bungalow, it was still evening. Putting their bags down, they went out to explore the surroundings. Badal said, "What a cock and bull story! There goes a deer, and I can see squirrels running about. A haunted forest, indeed!"

Neither Mainu, Tata nor Sonam had seen any deer or squirrels. But Badal had, hadn't he?

As the evening deepened, they came back. Badal said, "These sal trees are enormous! How much do you think they're worth?"

"Lakhs and lakhs of rupees."

"And so?"

"You're going to be a lakhpati!"

"Dear me, yes – I don't think I can help getting terribly rich. There's not much I can do about it!"

"Well, you could give some to us now and then!"

There were lights in the bungalow. The boys were somewhat surprised. There was a petromax lantern in the veranda, and one in the house. Who could have lit these? Approaching nearer, they had their answer. A girl sat on the veranda, an infant on her lap.

On seeing them, the girl laid down the child and stood up. Then she clasped her hands together and burst into tears.

The boys were more embarrassed than surprised, but a slightly relieved as well. Mainu said, "Please stop crying. You are Dhillon's wife, aren't you?"

"Yes, Babuji. This is my bungalow."

"Where have you been?"

"Where else could I be? I ran away to our village through the forest. The police create too many hassles. I do not understand a thing they say. How would I know that my husband would die? He doesn't like rituals and worship. So I fought with him and left with the baby. Then later, after what happened ... they would not let me stay at the village. They said, you married the Babu. Go to him. And when I came here, the police were after me."

"So you're the one who cleans up the house?"

"Yes, Babuji. Who else would?"

"How do you unlock it?"

"Here, with this master key. These keys can open up all the locks in this house. My baby is very sick. She is shrivelling up and refuses to eat anything. That is why I've been sitting here. I've decided that once it is morning, I shall go to the police officer myself. I'll tell him, I'll do whatever you ask, just take my baby to the hospital. I belong to the forest, I don't understand much. My husband did, and he would take care of everything. Babuji, may I please stay the night?"

"Of course, need you ask? You stay here with your baby. We'll be in that room. In the morning we shall ourselves take you there."

The girl returned after putting her baby to bed. She herself laid out their dinner. Kaka had packed some food for them. Despite repeated requests she did not join them, but she was quite forthcoming and told them a lot of things. She had no idea who had murdered Dhillon's nephew, Verma. She used to be so scared that she never came here. Now she visited occasionally because the villagers wouldn't let her stay.

The boys lay down in the living room. But how could sleep come to them? The mysteries of the forests of Jharowa now seemed to be resolved. The flaws in the girl's story had eluded them. Her glance had been so timid, her voice so full of tears.

Suddenly the girl cried out and they ran to her. "Babuji, Babuji! Why has my daughter gone limp? Please have a look. What will I do at this hour, where will I go?"

They scrambled up and ran to investigate. The baby, that three or four month old child, really seemed to be on the ebb. Badal was in front, the baby's mother kept pulling at his hand like a demented woman.

"Babuji, come closer. Touch her, tell me my daughter is alive!"

The perplexed Badal approached the baby. And the child, who had, till now, been lying as if dead, suddenly gurgled with laughter, and seemed to float up from the bed. She put her mouth to Badal's throat, sucking. Badal's voice choked in terror. His eyes popped out. Mainu and the others stood transfixed at this unbelievable sight. The girl held on to Badal and in the warm human voice of a doting mother said, "Drink your fill, my darling, drink, my pearl ..."

• In The Forests Of Jharowa •

Sonam broke out of his terrified trance, brought Badal's rifle and fired repeatedly at the girl. She did not even flinch. At some point she took up the baby and went out of the room. Badal collapsed.

At the sound of th shot Suja Singh and Kaka arrived. After that everything is hazy. Foggy, confused. All four of them had to be taken to the hospital. Badal, of course, was no longer alive.

Then, one day, some time later, they returned home.

They never mention the forests of Jharowa anymore. But, even today, they are terrified at the sight of a small baby. They will not lose this fear as long as they live.

No one has entered the forests of Jharowa ever since.

"Jharowar Jangale." From *Nirbahcita Bhuter Galpo*, ed Ranjit Chattopadhyay, Ananda Publishers Private Ltd, Calcutta, 1992.

Notes on Contributors

Rabindranath Tagore (1861-1941) One of the greatest Indian poets of the twentieth century, he was awarded the Nobel Prize for Literature for *Gitanjali* in 1913. Born in an aristocratic landlord family of Calcutta, Rabindranath was admitted to many schools, but did not complete any course. He was tutored at home in literature, music and the fine arts, and at seventeen sent to England to study law. He published his first piece at the age of thirteen; had several books of poems by eighteen; and was married by the age of twenty two. In 1901, he set up Visva Bharati which grew into a world reputed university at Santiniketan. He was awarded a Doctorate Degree from Calcutta University in 1914. In 1915, he was conferred the Knighthood, which he returned in 1919 under protest against British atrocities. His collected works run into several volumes of poetry, fiction, plays, dance-dramas, essays, letters, short stories and not less than two thousand songs most of which he himself set to tune. He has been widely translated into several languages.

Pramatha Chaudhuri (1868-1946) Born in East Bengal, educated at Calcutta and a Bar-at-Law from England, he taught at a Calcutta law college after a stint as estate manager to the Tagores. He contributed to Bangla literature by encouraging the use of more colloquial language. He edited *Sabuj Patra* magazine in 1914. Known for his short stories and humorous essays, he himself translated poetry from the European languages. A collection of fifty of his sonnets was published in 1913. In later life, he edited the Visva Bharati magazine.

Panchkari De (1873-1945) A noted writer, he had some thirty detective novels to his credit and was very well-known in his day. Some of his books have been translated into other Indian languages.

Bibhutibhushan Bandopadhyay (1894-1950) A school teacher throughout his life, and a prolific writer with nearly two hundred titles to his credit, he is noted for his depiction of the poverty, suffering, as well as the beauty of rural life in Bengal. Some of his stories and novels, such as *Pather Panchali* and *Asani Sanket,* have been made into well-known films by the famous director Satyajit Ray. He was awarded the Rabindra Memorial Prize posthumously in 1951 for his novel *Icchamati*.

Tarashankar Bandopadhyay (1898-1971) Immediately after leaving school and on entering college, he got involved in the freedom movement and was imprisoned for a year. After his release, he decided to devote his time to writing. Born in a family of landlords, he was fully conversant with the problems of Bengali peasants as also those of the feudal society. In most of his one hundred and thirty titles of fiction he dealt with the social transition of his time with immense sympathy for the poor and the deprived. In 1962 he was appointed Member of the Upper House of the State. He was awarded the Sahitya Akademi Puraskar in 1955 for his novel *Arogya Niketan* and the Rabindra Memorial Prize in 1956 for *Gana Debata*. In 1966, he received the Jnanpith. He was also felicitated with the Padmashri and the Padmabhushan by the Government of India for his service to literature. His works have been translated into many Indian languages.

Banaphul (1899-1979) Writing under the name Banaphul, Balaichand Mukhopadhyay began his literary career while studying medicine. After practising as a pathologist in Bhagalpur from 1939 to 1968, he moved to Calcutta. A prolific writer of fiction, he is famous for his classical novels *Dana, Sthabar* and *Jangam*. Many of his stories have been successfully filmed. Among many others, he was awarded the Rabindra Memorial Prize in 1962 for his novel *Haate Bajare*. He was also conferred the Padmabhushan in 1976.

Swapanburo (1902-1993) Writing under the name Swapanburo, Akhil Neogi was educated in the Government Art College, Calcutta, and started his career as a commercial artist. He then became a story writer, first for young readers in *Sishusathi* magazine, subsequently in *Jugantar*. He has about sixty published titles including sixteen plays. He was awarded several prizes for literature including the Vidyasagar Prize by the state government. He was also known as an organizer of children's festivals for which he formed a group Sab Peyechhir Asar.

Lila Majumdar (1908-) A distinguished scholar with a Master's degree, she was a lecturer for a while. A producer with the All India Radio, Calcutta, and well-known for her writings for young readers, she has been awarded the Rabindra Memorial and Vidyasagar Memorial prizes for excellence in juvenile literature. A translator, she also edited *Sandesh* magazine.

Kamakshiprasad Chattopadhyay (1917-1976) A well-known poet as also a fiction writer, both for children and adults, he was awarded the Bankim Gold Medal for his Bachelor's examinations. A representative for India at the PEN International at Venice in 1948, he lived in Moscow for several years to translate and edit the works of Gorky, Turgenev and Leo Tolstoy. An excellent photographer, he tried several other jobs before settling down to full-time writing and editing.

Shishir Lahiri (1924-) A Master's in Bangla literature, he wrote for eminent literary magazines like the *Desh* and published many novels and short stories.

Mahashweta Devi (1926-) Educated at Santiniketan, she taught English literature in a college for some time. A prolific writer, she is also a social activist working on behalf of marginalized tribal populations among the tribals of the border areas of Bihar and West Bengal. She was awarded the Sahitya Akademi Puraskar in 1979. She is also a recepient of the Magsaysay Award. Her works have been widely translated.

Suchitra Samanta Born in 1949, and raised for most of her life in India, she received her undergraduate degree from Calcutta University in English literature in 1968. She has a Master's in Drama and a Doctoral Degree in Cultural Anthropology from the University of Virginia in the USA. Her academic research, till 1998, has been on the Bengali religious experience of the goddess Kali and she has various published papers in academic journals on this topic. As of 1998, her field of research and writing is on the cultural obstacles to education faced by impoverished young girls living in a largely Muslim basti in Southern Calcutta.

The best of India translated.
– India Today

KATHA

MASTI
ED BY RAMACHANDRA SHARMA

Simple stories of ordinary men and women pulsate with life at Masti's masterly hand.
– *The Indian Express*

... immensely readable, gentle ...
– *The Pioneer*

MAUNI
ED BY LAKSHMI HOLMSTRÖM

The most sensitively edited and translated Indian book ... a dazzling collaboration of love.
– *Indian Review of Books*

... brilliant translations.
– *The Book Review*

BASHEER
ED BY VANAJAM RAVINDRAN

The aesthetically designed, and almost flawlessly printed book is a must for all those who are lovers of the exquisite and the brilliant in Indian literature.
– *The Hindustan Times*

... A celebration of the Indian experience in all its diversity.
– *The Express Magazine*

Katha's collection of short stories are a treasure, once again.
– *The Week*

Katha's work is of tremendous significance in building a new India.
– *Business Standard*

About Katha

Katha is a registered nonprofit organization working in the area of creative communication for development. Katha's main objective is to spread the love of books and the joy of reading amongst children and adults. Our activities span from publishing to education.

Kalpavriksham, Katha's Centre for Sustainable Learning, is active in the field of education. It develops and publishes quality material in the literacy to literature spectrum, and works with an eye to excellence in education – from nonformal education of working children to formal education, from primary through higher education. Katha also works with teachers to help them make their teaching more creative. It publishes learning packages for first-generation schoolgoers and adult neo-literates. Specially designed for use in nonformal education, every quarter Katha brings out *Tamasha!,* a fun and activity magazine on development issues for children, in Hindi and English. The *Katha Vachak* series is an attempt to take fiction to neo-literates, especially women. *Stree Katha* and *Stree Shakti* are illustrated, information-packed, interactive books on women's issues in a number of Indian languages.

Katha-Khazana, a part of Kalpavriksham, was started in Govindpuri, in one of Delhi's largest slum clusters, in 1990. Kathashala and the Katha School of Entrepreneurship have over 1300 students – mostly working children. To enhance their futures, an empowerment and income-generation programme for the women of this community – Shakti-Khazana – and adult literacy programme and advocacy groups were also started there, again in 1990.

Project Kanchi is Katha's effort to help forge linkages through academic interface programmes. It is working to develop syllabi and teaching material for courses in pedagogy, teaching translation, creative writing, fiction appreciation, management through fiction and culture linking. Launched in 1997, Kanchi has been conducting workshops in schools and colleges all over the country as part of this project. To further the objectives of this project, we have started an academic publishing programme – the **Approaches to Literature in Translation** series – as well as a Resource Centre for Teachers. Kanchi operates through four **Academic Centres** in various universities in the country – Bangalore University, North Eastern Hills University, Shillong, SNDT, Mumbai, in addition to its Delhi Centre.

Katha Vilasam, the Story Research and Resource Centre, seeks to foster and applaud quality fiction from the regional languages and take it to a wider readership through translations. The Katha Awards, instituted in 1990, are given annually to the best short fiction published in various languages that year, and for translations of these stories. Through projects like the All India and SAARC Translation Contests, it attempts to build a bank of sensitive translators. Katha Vilasam also functions as a literary agency and works with academia to associate students in translation-related activities. KathaNet, an invaluable network of Friends of Katha, is the mainstay of all Katha Vilasam efforts. Katha Vilasam publications also include exciting books in the Yuvakatha and Balkatha series, for young adults and children respectively.

Be a Friend of Katha!

If you feel strongly about Indian literature, you belong with us! KathaNet, an invaluable network of our friends, is the mainstay of all our translation-related activities. We are happy to invite you to join this ever-widening circle of translation activists. Katha, with limited financial resources, is propped up by the unqualified enthusiasm and the indispensable support of nearly 4000 dedicated women and men.

We are constantly on the lookout for people who can spare the time to find stories for us, and to translate them. Katha has been able to access mainly the literature of the major Indian languages. Our efforts to locate resource people who could make the lesser-known literatures available to us have not yielded satisfactory results. We are specially eager to find Friends who could introduce us to Bhojpuri, Dogri, Kashmiri, Maithili, Manipuri, Nepali, Rajasthani and Sindhi fiction.

Do write to us with details about yourself, your language skills, the ways in which you can help us, and any material that you already have and feel might be publishable under a Katha programme. All this would be a labour of love, of course! But we do offer a discount of 20% on all our publications to Friends of Katha.

Write to us at –
Katha
A-3 Sarvodaya Enclave
Sri Aurobindo Marg
New Delhi   110 017   Or call us at:686- 8193, 652-1752

Also from the House of Tamasha!
A fascinating tale of
The Princess with the Longest Hair

"...One silent night, Parineeta quickly left her room. Through empty passages and down dark staircases she reached a door in the palace wall and..."

Where did Parineeta go??
Get your copy today for Rs 120.

Other Books From The House Of Tamasha!

Crocodile And Other Stories
ISBN 81-85586-86-1

On A Sunny Shiny Night And Other Poems
ISBN 81-85586-87-X

Reach For The Moon!
ISBN 81-85586-88-8

The Elephant's Child And Other Stories
ISBN 81-85586-89-6

Tigers Forever And Other Poems
ISBN 81-85586-90-X

The World Around Us!
ISBN 81-85586-91-8

Price: Rs 25 each.
Special price: Rs 60 for a set of 3 books

Send your order to: Katha, A-3 Sarvodaya Enclave, Sri Aurobindo Marg, New Delhi 110 017.
Phone: 011-6868193 6521752 Fax: 011-6514373 E-mail: DELAAB05@giasdl01.vsnl.net.in